Writing to Richie

Writing to Richie

PATRICIA CALVERT

WITHDRAWN

CHARLES SCRIBNER'S SONS · NEW YORK
Maxwell Macmillan International · Toronto
Maxwell Macmillan International
New York · Oxford · Singapore · Sydney

Charles Scribner's Sons Books for Young Readers
Macmillan Publishing Company
866 Third Avenue, New York, NY 10022

Maxwell Macmillan Canada, Inc.
1200 Eglinton Avenue East, Suite 200
Don Mills, Ontario M3C 3N1

Macmillan Publishing Company is part of
the Maxwell Communication Group of Companies.

First edition   10 9 8 7 6 5 4 3 2 1
Printed in the United States of America

Library of Congress Cataloging-in-Publication Data
Calvert, Patricia.
Writing to Richie / by Patricia Calvert. — 1st ed.   p.   cm.
Summary: A tough-mannered girl who comes to live with David's new foster parents helps him come to terms with his younger brother's sudden death.
ISBN 0-684-19764-2
[1. Foster home care—Fiction.   2. Schools—Fiction.
3. Death—Fiction.   4. Brothers—Fiction.]   I. Title.
PZ7.C139Wr   1994   [Fic]—dc20   94-14458

For my grandsons,
Mickey Owen Elias
and Jacob George Halbert

Writing to Richie

Chapter One

"Richie?"

Richie kept his face turned away and refused to answer.

"Richie?" David hunched forward on the car seat, the better to peer sideways into his younger brother's face.

"Listen, Richie. This might be one of the best places ever. You listening to me, Richie?"

Richie said nothing.

"Maybe we'll get to stay a long time before we have to move again. Remember the Elliots? We were there practically—oh, it must've been practically a whole year. From one Christmas till almost the next one. Remember, Richie?"

Finally Richie turned. The smudges on his glasses made it hard for David to see the expression in his brother's eyes.

"Maybe it will, Richie," David persisted. "You can't tell. This might be practically the best place they ever put us."

They. For nearly as long as David could remember, the shape and order of life had been arranged by Theys.

Theys who were tall; Theys who were short. Theys who were men; Theys who were women. Old ones; young ones. A few who studied a person with shadows of pity in their glances; some who didn't want to look too closely for fear he and Richie might actually come into focus.

"That's what you always say, David," Richie objected. "You say those exact same words every single time. Only that's never how it turns out. Not really truly."

Richie didn't add *Why do you keep saying it when you know as well as me it never comes true?* but David knew that was exactly what his brother was thinking.

"Well, one thing for sure, we're still together," David reminded him because this time Richie seemed in need of some heavy-duty reminding. "They didn't split us up. Didn't send you one place, me somewhere else. If we always act right—don't ask for anything special, don't break any windows, don't pee in our beds— maybe they'll always leave you and me together."

The slope of his brother's shoulders told David that today Richie wasn't going to be comforted by any mights or maybes.

He scooted across the seat, closer to Richie's side. The seat covers in the Child Aid worker's car were plastic, which made sliding easier. He touched his brother's elbow, sharp and pointed as a stick in the sleeve of his size-too-large blue jacket.

"So anyway, Richie, you want to hear the story again?" he invited, softly, so the aid worker couldn't hear.

Like a sun rising over billowy summer treetops, a light slowly warmed Richie's eyes. "Sure," he said, his own voice low and soft too. "Maybe it won't come true, but I always like the way you tell it, David."

"In front there'll be this porch," David began. "Some chairs will be on it where you and me can sit when the weather gets warm." He'd told the story so often that he knew exactly what came next.

"In the backyard there'll be grass and a garden. In one corner there'll be this sandy place where we can play cars. We'll make roads and bridges and mountains and everything. In the summer there'll be carrots and corn and green beans, but no peas because me and you don't like peas."

David paused to savor the story himself.

"We'll have a room upstairs. There'll be two big beds this time, Richie, not those skinny little cots like some places we been, almost like you were in prison or something. A big bed for you, a big one for me." David sighed. "We'll get a box to put in the corner and we'll keep all our treasures in it."

The stuff about the treasures was Richie's favorite part. "What treasures?" he asked, his lips curving in a mild smile. He liked to have them listed, one by one.

"That green glass insulator cover we found down by the railroad tracks that day we walked home from Gramma's," David began. "The seashell Mrs. Gregory gave us that when you hold it up to your ear has still got the sound of the ocean in it." David smiled himself, remembering that mellow roar.

"That old tin can with the hinged lid and a picture of Prince Albert on the front," he went on. "Uncle Paulie's hood ornament from the old Pontiac. Our three race cars, and the stuffed bear you got at the Goodwill for twenty-five cents whose eye fell out when we were at the Krulwiches."

"All our treasures," Richie echoed, his own eyes pleased and dim behind his dirty glasses. "They'll all be in one place, and we can touch 'em anytime we want. Yeah. Maybe this'll be one of the best places ever."

Then he added a fresh, unexpected touch of his own. "These new people might even have a dog," he speculated.

"Jeez, Richie! They better not," David warned.

Richie was silent for three blocks. "I hope they do," he insisted. His voice was flat and full of resistance. He folded his shoulders into himself like a bird folding its wings.

"Yeah, right!" David snorted softly. "And you won't be in that house five minutes before you start to sneeze. Five minutes later your eyes'll start to water and get all swoll up till they're only teeny slits you can't hardly see out of. Your nose'll turn red and begin to drip. Pretty soon you'll start to hack. Next thing, you'll have to get out your inhaler. Forget it, Richie. It happens every time you get near anything with hair on it."

Richie's mild smile turned sly and fiendish. "You got hair, David. I never sneeze around you." He turned away to stare out of the window again.

"Don't be a wisenheimer," David grumbled. "You know darn good'n well what I mean."

He knew Richie did too. The doctors said he had allergies. It meant cats and dogs and house dust and pollen and pillow feathers—would you believe even something like cake flour?—made Richie sneeze his fool head off.

With all the science in the world—sending people

4

fathoms under the ocean in big metal cages so they could study sharks up close or into space to repair that Hubble telescope so astronomers could look back to the beginning of time—with great science like that, wouldn't you think somebody could invent a simple thing like a dog that didn't make a person sneeze?

David tried to imagine what such an animal might look like. Kind of naked, not having any hair, he decided. You'd have to buy it one of those little sweaters to keep it from feeling embarrassed when you took it out for a walk. You might even have to write a letter to the Day's End Senior Center and ask Gramma to knit a special cap with little holes so its ears could poke through, maybe even a pair of shoes so its bare feet didn't get cold.

David sighed again, and stared out the window too.

"Somewhere I bet there is one," he heard Richie mutter.

"One what?"

"An animal that doesn't make a person sneeze."

"Forget it, Richie," David groaned. "A dog is a dumb idea. We got trouble enough already."

Richie huddled against the car window and flattened his nose against the glass.

David was sorry he'd used those words, *dumb* and *trouble*. That was mean. Now Richie would feel worse than ever.

The thing was, it was hard to be a mom and a dad and a brother to Richie all at the same time. Sometimes you made mistakes. Said things that were sharp and hurtful. David decided to switch back to their former conversation, the one in which he'd tried to remind Richie of their blessings.

5

"This might be the best place they ever put us, Richie. You can't tell. Might be. Because we're still together. That's what counts, Richie."

Still together. To make sure Richie got the message, David repeated everything he'd just said.

Richie didn't answer. He pressed his nose flatter on the glass. Soon a halo of fog circled his head. In the front seat, Mr. Hutton turned to announce, "We're almost there, boys. It won't be long now."

We're almost there. It won't be long now.

David couldn't count how many times he'd heard those words before. They'd been said so often that they made a lie out of everything he'd just been trying to tell Richie.

Chapter Two

Fifteen minutes later, Mr. Hutton pulled up to the curb under a large oak tree that wore a skirt of sparkly February snow around its bottom.

Richie sat up straight on the car seat, as if he'd been goosed in the ribs. "Look, David," he whispered. He pointed.

David looked. What was that standing there on the porch beside the new foster lady? It looked like a dog. It *was* a dog. Not large, not small; just sort of a dog-sized dog. It had hair. Quite a lot of it, actually, most of it the color of warm butterscotch.

"What's that?" Richie asked. Amazement made his voice sound hollow, as if he were talking through the wall of a closet. When they lived with the Krulwiches, Richie had spent a lot of time in a corner of a closet in the downstairs hallway. He said he liked it in there, where it was dark and quiet with only umbrellas and snow boots for company.

"What does it look like, doofus?" David felt amazement bloom reluctantly under his own ribs.

"A dog."

"Shoosh. What an IQ. I bet you could make a kazillion bucks on *Jeopardy*."

"I wonder what its name is?" Richie murmured, mostly to himself.

"Wendell," Mrs. Birk told them when they stood on the porch a few minutes later beside the Child Aid worker. "His name's Wendell."

Mrs. Birk smiled, and seemed a bit embarrassed. "I'll admit it's a rather foolish name to give a dog. The truth is, I had a cousin once who looked exactly like him. Sort of sweet, you know. The minute I saw this pooch down at the animal shelter, I said to Mr. Birk, 'Why, that dog reminds me a lot of my cousin Wendell out there in Dubuque, Iowa.'"

She smoothed her skirt, which was dark blue and had a blizzard of white daisies on it. "That Wendell's dead now, but this one's still quite alive."

David could see that for himself. A knot tightened in his belly as he waited for Richie to start sneezing. For his nose to drip and turn red. For his eyes to water and get so puffy that they were narrow little slits in his face. For his cough to start. For him to reach, gasping and breathless, into his jacket for his inhaler.

Nothing happened.

Had someone invented a dog that didn't make a person sneeze? David wondered if part of the magic was because this dog was named after somebody's cousin who lived in Dubuque, Iowa.

"My brother has allergies," he announced anyway, just in case it was a fluke, that Richie's cure turned out not to be permanent.

"Yes, I know," Mrs. Birk said, and smiled again. Her hair was white, and she looked a lot older than most foster mothers, which was something of a disappointment. "The placement people told me. Maybe Richie will be able to get along with Wendell, though. You see, Wendell is mostly poodle. That means he doesn't shed his hair, or at least hardly ever. But I promise that if Richie has any trouble at all, why, Mr. Birk will just move Wendell down to the basement while you boys are with us."

David could tell by the look on Richie's face that his brother was imagining Wendell in the basement. There would be spiders down there, he knew Richie was thinking. Mice too, probably. Sometimes there were even lizards and beetles in basements, and the corners would be all dark and cobwebby. For a minute Richie looked as if he might sneeze or cry, but he didn't do either one.

"Wendell was here first," Richie pointed out. "It wouldn't be fair to stick him in the basement." David wondered if Wendell didn't smile behind his butterscotch whiskers to hear he'd been offered a reprieve from cobwebs and lizards.

David felt the Child Aid worker's hand on his shoulder, steering him into the house. Beside him, Richie walked stiffly, his eyes dim but victorious behind his dirty glasses.

"They got a dog, David, and I never sneezed once," he whispered triumphantly.

In Mrs. Birk's kitchen, Mr. Hutton spread his papers all over the table. Mrs. Birk served some brownies sprinkled with powdered sugar. David took only one and held back Richie's hand when his brother reached for seconds.

"The boys come from a rather unfortunate background," Mr. Hutton explained. "Their mother is only periodically able to care for them. She's in and out of various treatment centers due to some severe emotional problems."

David was sure he could have told the story better himself.

For instance, he could usually always tell when Mom was going into a new bad time. It was as if she couldn't hear what you were trying to tell her. As if she was off in a world of her own. Her smile stayed mild—it was a lot like Richie's, warm but vague—and she'd never been the sort of mentally ill person to commit wild or dangerous acts. It was mostly as if she just went away into a room somewhere up there in her head, turned the key, and locked the door behind her. David wondered sometimes what color that room was painted, if it had windows and curtains and furniture in it. It must have been comfortable in there because you never knew for sure if she'd come out again, or when.

"The boys' father doesn't work steadily enough to provide an appropriate home for his sons," Mr. Hutton went on, "and alcohol has often been a problem."

Well, yes, David thought, that was true. Dad would buy a twelve-pack of beer and sometimes didn't quit drinking until he'd stacked the empties pyramid-style beside the couch, as if he were trying to build a wall around himself. By the time he was three-fourths of the way through the twelve-pack, he was so sloshed he couldn't pop the top of another one. And when he wasn't drinking, he seemed sad and never looked straight at you, but somewhere up over the top of your head or past your left ear.

"However, David and Richie have never been serious

behavior problems in any of the other homes we've placed them, so you shouldn't have any trouble," Mr. Hutton concluded, shuffling his papers and frowning.

"Of course, you know our policy, Mrs. Birk. It seems best not to leave children too long in one location," he warned. "It's wise to avoid letting either the foster parents or the children become overly attached or dependent on each other because sooner or later changes always have to be made."

Tell me about it, David agreed silently. Richie and me may not know much, but for sure we know all about the Policy.

Mrs. Birk told the aid worker she'd been a foster parent many times before, and that she'd do the best she could for whatever time the boys were with her.

"I'm sure we'll get along just fine, Mr. Hutton," she finished. "Robert and I have cared for, oh, probably more than thirty children over the years." David watched her carefully; some foster parents were nice in front of the placement workers but not so nice after they left. It was way too early to tell which kind Mrs. Birk would turn out to be.

After Mr. Hutton was gone, Mrs. Birk invited them upstairs to see their room. The house was old and the stairs were narrow, but once you got up to the second floor, everything was light and airy. There were two rooms separated from each other by a small hall. She directed them into the larger one.

"Sometimes we have two children on this side and another one across the hall," she said. "For a while, though, I think we'll have only you boys. Now that Mr. Birk and I are older, we think two children will be quite enough for us."

11

The room was plainer than some they'd stayed in. The linoleum on the floor, printed with green leaves the size of elephants' ears, was worn through in spots to the tar-paper backing, but was waxed to a shine. There were two beds, large ones, an arm's length apart. Each one had two pillows. In the corner was a box. It was made of wood and had a lid with a rope handle.

"What's in that box?" Richie asked.

"It's empty," Mrs. Birk said. "I thought you boys might have things to put in it. A toy or two, perhaps, that you'd been able to bring with you. The boys and girls who've stayed with us before seemed to enjoy having a safe place to put their special things. Sometimes they brought books or stuffed animals. Seems like most all of them had something dear."

Something dear. The words sounded nice put together like that.

Mrs. Birk smoothed the bedspreads, which were already smooth. She plumped up the pillows, which were already plump.

"It will soon be time for lunch, boys," she said. "I'll go downstairs and put some on, and will call you when it's ready. There's a bathroom at the end of the hall where you can wash up. Meantime, you can get yourselves settled and decide who will sleep in which bed."

Richie sat carefully on the edge of the bed he'd decided would be his.

"There's a box for our treasures, David, just like in your story," he said. He studied the four corners of the room. "Even though this room isn't as fancy as the one at the Krulwiches', I sort of like it better," he declared.

David went to the window, then beckoned to Richie. "Look down there," he said. Below, in one corner of the yard, was what seemed to be a small sandy spot where—if you wanted to—you could build roads and bridges and mountains for cars to race over. In the sunniest part of the yard were the ruined remains of last summer's garden, but from so far away it was hard to tell if any of the plants had been peas.

"What if you were right, David?" Richie breathed softly. "What if this turns out to be the best place ever? What if Mr. Hutton practically forgets where he put us? What if . . . ?"

David laid his fingers lightly over Richie's lips.
"Don't say anything more," he warned. "We'll just be glad we're here. For however long that turns out to be. And maybe the next time they come to get us, they'll say Mom is lots better and Dad doesn't buy twelve-packs anymore." It was a dream he'd never stopped dreaming, not from the very first time he and Richie went into foster care.

"Right now, we won't make any plans, Richie. For now, we'll just . . ." David paused. "We'll just try to be."

Chapter Three

Not everything could be just left to be, of course.

Certain things needed to be taken care of right away. Mrs. Birk announced at breakfast the next morning that since they were entering school in the middle of the year, the first thing that needed to be done was to get registered.

"We'll go over to Franklin Elementary this morning," she said as she buttered some toast and set out marmalade and strawberry jam. She put two large yellow bowls and a box of cornflakes on the table.

"We can get your room assignments and a list of the supplies you boys will need," she said. "Then we can go over to the mall, and by tomorrow—that will be Wednesday—you'll be ready for your first full day at your new school."

So many new schools, David thought. So many first days when he and Richie were the new kids. Having done it so often before, you'd think it would get easier and easier, but it never did. Starting late, after all the other kids were used to one another and had made alliances of twos and threes and fours (sometimes, alliances were defended by pushes and shoves against an invader) made being new scary every time.

David expected they'd go out the back door into the garage, where Mrs. Birk would start the car—he'd seen Mr. Birk ride away earlier on a bicycle to go to his job at the UPS office—but instead, she put on her coat and beckoned them onto the front porch.

"Franklin is only four blocks away," she explained, "and the mall is only four blocks farther." She walked like a person who enjoyed it, David noticed, and swung her arms at her sides like someone in a parade.

"When it was first built—the mall, I mean—Mr. Birk and I didn't like it at all," she went on. "We missed the lovely green field with its pretty brown cows and white daisies that used to be where the mall is now. But we got used to the change. Now, we sometimes go over just to watch the people or to get ice-cream cones."

"Do you think you'll get ice-cream cones today?" Richie's question clearly wasn't a question at all but a suggestion, so David pinched him hard. They'd been with the Birks for less than a day; it was way too soon to ask for anything special, even an ice-cream cone.

Sometimes, after you got to know fosters better, you realized the time would never be right to ask them for anything. Somehow, Richie never could get it through his head that you had to be careful about stuff like that.

"Well, we might," Mrs. Birk said.

Richie smirked, and David didn't resist when he got pinched back. Hard.

Franklin Elementary was newer than some of the schools they'd gone to, and the floors hadn't had a chance to get too scarred up yet. The paint on the lockers was fresh, and from the smell that wafted up the hall, David knew there'd be Beanie Weenie casserole for lunch. He hated Beanie Weenie casserole, but the smell made his stomach juices flow, which made him look forward himself to a possible ice-cream cone at the mall.

In the school office, Mrs. Birk greeted the woman behind the counter as if she was accustomed to coming here often.

"These are my new boys," she announced, and sounded pleased to be able to introduce them. "This is David," she said, and David felt her rest her hand lightly on his head. "And this is Richard. Their last name is Haywood. Boys, this is Miss Pritchett. Now, Miss P., we'd like to register this morning and get a list of the supplies the boys will need."

David resisted the temptation to be too hopeful, but it sounded nice the way Mrs. Birk said *we*.

After they got the lists, they walked past the room where Richie would go tomorrow. "We won't disturb the class this morning," Mrs. Birk whispered, "but I just wanted you to have a chance to see what it looks like from the outside." Later, David got to see his room, too, which, since he was two grades ahead, was at the opposite end of the building.

As they turned down the hall to leave, a tall boy passed and David turned to watch him go into the room that tomorrow would be his own as well.

The boy turned, too, just before he went through the door, and David recognized what he saw. Trouble.

Jeez. Some kids wore it like they wore their name-brand jeans or favorite sweatshirts. It was there, part of them, even more obvious than their eye color or having straight or curly hair. Trouble. David felt his heart shrink, and a familiar cramping sensation seized his bowels.

At the mall, Mrs. Birk let them select the color of the notebooks they needed. Richie always picked yellow. "It's the color of the sun," he liked to say. This time, David took blue. A good color to go with Richie's sun.

There was something about a new notebook that was so promising. Its pages were sleek and empty, and in the beginning David always had hopes for such notebooks, as if in their pages he'd find out something important about himself, would find a special message intended only for him. He never did, but somehow the promise was always there in those smooth, unblemished pages.

At a place called The Creamery Mrs. Birk bought double-dippers, chocolate and vanilla. By the time they got home, the cones were gone, and she suggested they might like to take Wendell for a walk around the block. She got a leash out of the coat closet in the front hall and hooked it onto Wendell's collar.

"It will give the three of you a chance to get better acquainted," she said, "but be sure to let me know if Richie takes to sneezing or has any sort of problem at all."

They'd gotten nearly the full way around the block before Richie sneezed even once. "Hey, David, it isn't Wendell's fault," he said, wiping his nose on his sleeve. "Remember, that doctor said I was allergic to grass and mold and a whole bunch of other stuff. Look at the bark on that tree. It's got mold on it, David, thicker'n a sweater! I'm pretty sure my problem isn't Wendell." Wendell wagged his tail, and even seemed to smile.

It wasn't mold on the tree, David knew, only lichen, but he allowed himself to believe Richie was right about Wendell. "Just the same, you better not pet him," he warned as Richie reached to stroke Wendell's ears, and took the leash just to be on the safe side. Wendell switched over to walk amiably on David's side of the sidewalk, and didn't seem offended to hear that he couldn't be petted.

"Hey. You scared about tomorrow?" Richie asked. The question was sudden, but David knew Richie had probably been thinking about it all day.

"I'm always scared," David admitted. Since he was two grades ahead, he'd had a longer time to live with that feeling than Richie, but somehow he never got over the heart-shrinking, gut-cramping dread that a new school always caused him to have.

"Me too," Richie agreed. "Do you think it'll ever be different?"

"Will what be different?"

"That you and me won't be scared anymore."

"Someday. Maybe." David reached down to stroke Wendell's ears. He remembered the boy back at Franklin Elementary who had trouble written all over him. But probably not this time, he realized. Not this time.

Chapter Four

David had planned to hold Richie's hand all the way to school, but after they waved good-bye to Mrs. Birk he decided not to. If he did, he reasoned, the kid might get spooked.

Today, neither of them mentioned anything about being scared, and twenty minutes later David watched his brother go into his new classroom without a squawk. Richie's back was straight, his eyes dim and steady behind the smudged lenses of his glasses, which Mrs. Birk had gotten only half clean with a dish towel just before they left the house.

David remembered the first day of school when they'd lived with the Krulwiches. Richie lay on the floor outside his first-grade room and refused to move. When the teacher tried to pick him up, he got all stiff and glassy-eyed. She laid him down again, fearing he might be having some sort of fit.

The school nurse came to take his pulse and make sure his breathing was regular. It was best to let him be, she advised. At recess, everyone had to step over him. He lay there like a fallen log till lunch. He must've been

19

starving (David recalled that the hallway had smelled richly of pizza that noon, Richie's favorite food), but in spite of it he'd never budged.

They'd gone to two schools that year too, David remembered, and in the next one Richie huddled under his desk for almost a week. Mrs. Morgan (the lady who came after Mrs. Krulwich) was called to school twice for counseling sessions with the principal. By the second week Richie sat at his desk part of the day, but when he felt gloomy or upset he still crawled underneath it and sat there with bowed head, as if he were doing some kind of magic.

As soon as David stepped into his own new classroom he glanced around quickly, wondering if the first face that would show itself in that galaxy of unfamiliar moons would be the one belonging to Trouble.

The boy from yesterday was nowhere to be seen. David felt a heavy weight rise from his shoulders. Maybe he'd been mistaken. Maybe that kid was a monitor from an upper grade (he'd been tall enough to be). Maybe he didn't belong in this class at all.

"Boys and girls, I want to introduce our new student to you," the teacher announced in a voice that glowed brightly with primary colors. "This is David Haywood, and I want all of you to give him a warm welcome."

There was a small collective sigh from the class, a sound like air being let out of a balloon, then two or three weak "Hi, David"s escaped to hang up near the light fixtures.

"David has a brother in—" Mrs. Olson turned to him eagerly. "Can you tell us what grade he's in, David?"

David knew Mrs. Olson's invitation was a way of making him speak up. When you'd been a new kid so often, you began to recognize certain things, little techniques and ploys that teachers and fosters used to get you settled in.

"Third," he said. "His name's Richie."

"David has a brother named Richie who's in third grade," Mrs. Olson echoed in her warm red-yellow-and-blue voice, then directed him to a desk at the back of the room. Everything about the desk was new and fresh, like the school itself, and David felt a tingle of anticipation. He was in the middle of arranging his notebook and paper and pencils when the door opened.

In walked Trouble.

David felt that familiar weight descend once more onto his shoulders, back, and neck. Worse, Trouble plopped something onto Mrs. Olson's desk, then shambled back to where David felt himself wrinkling and shrinking at his desk that only a moment before had filled him with hope. Trouble folded himself into the desk right across the aisle.

"Evan, your new classmate is David Haywood. David, meet Evan Ellis," Mrs. Olson said. "Evan, why don't you show David where we are in our social studies book?"

With a weary groan, as if he were often asked to perform chores beyond what ought to be requested of him, Evan reached across the aisle, took David's copy of *The World and Its People,* and flipped it open to chapter 2.

"We're doing Egypt now," he sighed in a voice that was soft and hard at the same time. He pointed at a picture of a pyramid. "Not much over there but camels and sand."

"Thanks," David murmured.

Perhaps he'd misjudged the look he thought he'd seen yesterday. Evan Ellis seemed to be a boy who was too tired to make trouble. In spite of his fears, maybe everything would be okay this time.

At nine-forty-five everyone leaped up and tore out of the room, down the hall, out to the playground. Recess was always a problem when you were a new kid, and the way Child Aid ran things—moving you so quick, before you had a chance to fit in—you never got over being new.

David stayed in his chair and looked at the pictures in *The World and Its People.*

"Come along, David," Mrs. Olson urged. "You need a breath of fresh air, too." She waited, smiling but tapping her foot, and David saw that she intended to lock the classroom behind her so that she could go to have coffee with the other teachers. He sighed, and shuffled outdoors.

Evan was playing tetherball with two other boys, who weren't nearly as tall as he was. If you were a big kid, did that automatically mean you were a mean kid too? Maybe so; most of the mean kids David had known had always been at least a head taller than he was himself.

"Ya wanna play?" Evan hollered across the playground. David felt torn by doubt. Should he take a chance? He hung against the wall, grateful for how solid it felt against his backbone. He shook his head.

"You too good for us or you chicken or what?" Evan demanded, and gave the ball a whack as if he were in training for an upcoming Golden Gloves bantamweight match.

David shrugged. He studied his feet. Big mistake. He

should've agreed to play, he realized, whether he was in the mood or not. How to explain that he hadn't meant to be rude, that he was only being careful? Of course, people like Evan Ellis never had to be careful about anything.

"Tomorrow," he called back. "I'll play tomorrow."

"Won't ask ya tomorrow," Evan promised in his silky, soft-hard voice.

On the way home, Richie seemed almost happy with the way his day had gone. "My teacher is nice," he reported. "Her name's Miss Parker. I told her about my allergies and everything. She says she'll help me be careful of chalk dust and stuff like that. She even told the class I had allergies. One girl—I think her name was Amanda—said her big sister has 'em, too. Sometimes she has to have extra oxygen and even has to go to the hospital like I did that one time."

David listened with only half an ear. He still felt preoccupied with what had happened at recess. Then, on the corner, he spied Evan Ellis. Since he was almost a head taller than anyone else, you couldn't miss him.

"Let's go this way," he suggested to Richie, and turned hastily down a street that had houses on it that were even smaller and more modest than Mrs. Birk's.

"Why?" Richie wanted to know, trotting alongside.

"There's a guy back there," David said.

"One of them guys who makes trouble?"

"You got it."

Richie was silent for a moment. "Sometimes I think it's us," he said. "There's something about you and me that makes kids like him be mean to us, David."

The possibility had already crossed David's mind, but he shook his head. "Don't be crazy, Richie. We're new.

23

And smaller. That's all. Big kids always pick on littler kids. Long as I can remember I've been one of the littlest kids in my class. Long as I can remember I've been picked on too."

Yet it had occurred to him that maybe somehow he and Richie *were* branded, that even before other kids found out they were in foster care, they just knew.

Once, he'd peered at himself in a mirror (at the Krulwiches'? the Elliots'?) and had passed his hand across his forehead to make sure nothing was written there in raised bumps, like Braille, that other people could read if the light hit your face just right. Another time, he checked the back of his shirt to make sure no message had been pasted there or woven mysteriously into the fabric. Weird. Somehow, people just *knew.*

When they turned the corner and Mrs. Birk's white porch was clearly in sight, suddenly so was Evan Ellis. He'd sneaked around from the opposite direction, and now blocked the sidewalk with a wide-legged stance.

"You two guys stuck up or something?" he asked amiably. The truth was, his face wasn't really mean. If anything, it was open and wide, and a smile seemed to linger just behind his mild, friendly blue eyes. Evan's cronies snickered as if the question was witty.

"No," David assured him. "I just wanted to show Richie a new way home."

Before he could think of what to say next, Evan looped five strong fingers around his wrist, and David felt his arm being cranked up between his shoulder blades. It happened so fast. That kind of stuff usually did.

"Sure you ain't stuck up?" Evan inquired patiently.

"Uh, sure," David heard himself grunt.

Evan applied a little more torque. "Positive?" he murmured agreeably.

David felt his chest tighten with pain and dread. "Positive," he croaked, sorry that his voice sounded so small and pinched. He knew Richie was watching, eyes huge and panicky behind the grunge on his glasses.

"Absolutely, totally positive?" Evan persisted tenderly, as he applied additional pressure.

"Absolutely. Totally." David felt tears sting his eyes. His voice was as thin as a shoelace. Half a block away he saw Mrs. Birk step onto her porch and stand there, shading her eyes against the clear spring sunshine.

Evan saw her, too, and gave David's arm a final quick, painful crank upward. "We'll discuss it another time, dude," he sighed in David's ear. As he passed, he gave Richie's glasses a tweak. "Jeez, kid, how d'you see through them bottle bottoms?" he asked with an amused snort.

"Shut your great big ugly fat face!" Richie screeched, suddenly brave because Mrs. Birk had stepped off her porch and was marching briskly up the street.

"*You* shut yours!" David hissed. "Don't make it worse than it already is, Richie!"

"How was school, boys?" Mrs. Birk asked with a smile. She apparently hadn't seen what Evil Evan had just done. The sun turned each hair on her head into a tiny silver corkscrew, and the expression in her brown eyes made it clear she was actually happy to see them.

"Fine," David said quickly, giving Richie a poke in the side. "We like it fine, don't we, Richie?"

"Well, I've made a fresh batch of peanut-butter cookies," she said. "Why don't you boys come have some with a glass of chocolate milk?"

Richie ate four and would've taken a fifth, but Mrs. Birk urged him not to ruin his supper. David ate only one. His stomach was still knotted with fear and regret.

Fear because he knew he'd get his arm cranked between his shoulder blades again. Maybe tomorrow even. Regret because he hadn't been able to stand up to Evan Ellis. It was always the same, he realized, grieving over the echo in his ears of his thin-as-a-shoelace voice. Always the same.

Chapter Five

"The boys had a good day at school," Mrs. Birk told Mr. Birk at supper. It was still too early to be sure, but David decided that even with white hair, she might be one of the better foster mothers. Her cookies were soft in the middle, the way he liked them, and she was willing to let you talk about stuff if you wanted to talk about it, but didn't hassle you if you were silent. Most of all, he liked the easy way she said "the boys."

Mr. Birk had a story to tell about his own day at the UPS office. "A package came in this morning, and right away it made me a little nervous," he reported. "When I went to pick it up off the loading dock, it seemed a lot heavier at one end than the other, but the minute I hoisted it up, by gosh, it was the opposite end that felt heavy." He paused, and drew his brows together. "I set it on the sorting shelf; that's when I heard the noise coming from inside."

Richie's eyes got round; his spoon, loaded with mashed potatoes, hung in midair. "What kind of noise?" he asked.

"A soft, scratchy noise. Like the sound tall grass

makes when it rubs against a pair of brand-new jeans that are stiff because they haven't been washed yet. That kind of rustling sound, you know?"

David saw Richie nod as if he knew exactly the sound Mr. Birk was talking about, which of course couldn't be true. As far back as David could remember, he and Richie had worn secondhand jeans from places like Goodwill or the Clothes Connection, jeans that some other kid had worn so long and so hard that the material was as soft and silent as flannel.

"I went to get the supervisor," Mr. Birk confided, lowering his voice. "These days, with people doing such crazy things to folks they don't even know, there was no telling what might be in that box. How could I be sure that someone didn't have a grudge against the UPS?"

The question hovered in the air, and Mr. Birk squinted at his audience.

"Of course, I couldn't open the package myself," he confessed. "That would be against department regulations. Only the supervisor could decide to do that." He ate a mouthful of potatoes and took a swallow of coffee.

David felt himself getting interested, too. Maybe it was a bunch of mercury in that package. He'd broken a thermometer once, and the stuff rolled out in little beads. It was strangely heavy too, but the minute you tried to catch it, the beads ran away from you and always headed for the low end of whatever you tried to catch them with before they melted back into one heavy silver blob again.

"'I don't think we need to call the bomb squad, Bob, but we'd better open 'er up,' the super told me."

Richie hunched forward, frozen to his chair, his chin level with his plate.

"So I did. Carefully. With the super looking on, which made it legal. I didn't much fancy looking over the edge of the box, let me tell you, but when I did, guess what I saw?"

"What?" Richie asked. His voice sounded scratchy, as if he were about to have an allergy attack.

Mr. Birk paused for effect. "It was a . . . a . . . *snake!*"

Mrs. Birk shrieked and put her hand over her mouth. "You might've been killed!" she exclaimed indignantly. "And you only three years from retirement!"

"A . . . *snake*?" Richie echoed.

"What kind?" David couldn't help asking.

"It was a boa constrictor that someone had ordered," said Mr. Birk, pleased by his audience's attention. "It was a young one, only about three feet long. Jack Wilson, who handles outgoing packages at the other end of the building—his cousin works in a pet store and hears a lot of stuff about animals—he said boas can get to be eighteen feet long and weigh two or three hundred pounds. Imagine! What made the package feel peculiar was that the snake moved every time I moved the box, to whichever end felt low to it."

Richie smiled with relief. "But everything turned out all right," he said. "You didn't get hurt at all."

Everything turned out all right. David liked the way those words sounded. For a moment, he forgot about Evan Ellis. In the Birks' kitchen, having eaten pork chops and mashed potatoes, having listened to a story about a boa, then watching Mrs. Birk get ice cream and chocolate syrup out of the fridge while Wendell waited

29

near the table's edge for a few scraps, his eyes sweet and patient beneath his butterscotch bangs, David decided it *was* possible that sometimes things could turn out all right.

At eight-fifteen the next morning, though, he realized he'd been mistaken. Evan Ellis didn't even wait for the day to get fully started before he resumed David's initiation to Franklin Elementary.

"There's that kid again," Richie pointed out when they were only half a block from Mrs. Birk's porch. "The one who ambushed us yesterday."

Evil Evan Ellis. The name had a certain musical zing to it.

"Don't worry," David told Richie. There was no sense both of them being scared poopless. "Listen, Richie. You go down that street we came home on yesterday. You can't get lost. I'll handle this guy by myself."

He had to push Richie down the street, though. "Hurry," he ordered, his voice getting that shoestring sound in it again. "You'll be at the playground in about two secs." Then he turned to face whatever early-morning harassment Evan had planned for him. Evil Ellis. Awful Evan. Icky Evan Ellis.

"So who's the little squirt?" Evan inquired in the tender way David realized he was doomed to become very used to. Then he remembered: Evan hadn't been in the room yesterday when Mrs. Olson revealed that he and Richie were brothers.

"None of your business," he said, his bowels tying themselves in knots.

"*Every*thing is my business," Evan purred. His voice

was mild, soft. "I *make* it my business," he added pleasantly. "One more time: Who's the kid?"

"He's staying at the same place I am. I don't know him too well, though."

Evan seemed genuinely surprised. "What d'you mean, 'staying at the same place'? Most kids stay home, not at *a place*."

David could see he'd made a mistake. To admit he was a foster now might only make things worse. But it was true—and anyway, Evan would find out sooner or later. "We're staying with Mrs. Birk. She takes in . . . uh . . . ah . . . foster kids."

Evan smiled with satisfaction. "I knew it. You guys always look the same. Like every night's Halloween and there's a spook behind every bush."

David shrugged and turned to head toward school.

"Hey! I'm not through talking to you yet," Evan warned. "I wanna know something. Like, what's it like, you know, being a foster and all? I never asked those other guys the Birks kept. Now I'm asking *you*."

David knew that even if he could tell Evan, the kid would never understand. If Evan thought Egypt was famous only for camels and sand, for sure he wouldn't understand anything about being a foster.

David lifted a shoulder. "It's okay. I got no complaints. Me and Richie are together. The placement people never separated us, not once. That's what counts."

Evan smirked. "I thought you said you didn't know the little turkey. So. He's your brother, huh?"

David scuffed the toe of his shoe against the sidewalk. "I didn't say he was my brother. I just said we were together at the Birks'. We been in a couple other foster homes at the same time."

Evan gave him a little shove. "Yeah, right." The next shove was loaded with more energy, and David slipped off the curb. "Guys like you are losers. You got it written all over you, you know that?"

So that's what showed. *Loser* was written all over him. Richie too, probably. When he'd looked in the mirror at the Krulwiches' and the Elliots' he'd never seen what others saw, but Evan, with his keen and piercing eye, hadn't been deceived.

Having found out David's true identity, Evan seemed to lose interest. "Aw, beat it," he ordered. "Kid like you ain't even worth getting detention for."

David walked slower and slower, hoping to put some distance between himself and his tormentor, which only made Evan irritable. "I said *beat it*," the bigger boy snapped. David leaped past Evan and broke into a trot.

"Double time!" Evan hollered. "Lemme see you do double time, kid!" David ran a little faster.

Suddenly, he hated everything. He burned with rage at Franklin Elementary, the Birks, the placement service, Richie, Mrs. Olson, hairy old Wendell. Life was full of people who snapped their fingers. Do this; do that. Jump higher. Run faster. Like it or not, you always did too.

One thing you could never do, though. You could never be who you really were. David knew it was already too late to find out who he was. He'd never know. He'd always be what someone else wanted him to be.

Richie had another good day at school. "We went to the auditorium for a film," he announced on the way home.

"It was about the en-vi-ron-ment. How to take care of garbage the right way. You're supposed to separate paper from plastic and put bottles and tin cans—wash 'em first so they don't attract rodents—in a different place."

Upstairs, after they'd each had a brownie and a glass of milk in the kitchen, Richie, who was still pleased with his day, had an idea. "You know all our treasures, David?" He lifted the lid of the wooden box in the corner and peered down at them as he spoke.

"What about 'em?" All David could think about was that Evan had said he wasn't even worth getting detention for.

"Let's set them on the windowsill where we can look at 'em all the time," Richie suggested. Without waiting for an answer, he began to remove the treasures and to space them evenly across the windowsill. Lastly, the one-eyed bear was propped up against the frame. Richie stood back to admire his arrangement.

"This way, we don't have to dig them out of the box when we want to see 'em or touch 'em," he explained. "First thing when we wake up tomorrow, there they'll be. Last thing at night, they'll still be there."

David had to admit the treasures looked nice the way Richie had placed them. A breeze coming through the window riffled the shaggy hair on the bear's head, and later, after he and Richie were in bed, the streetlight near the alley shone through the green glass insulator cover, making it seem like a real treasure, something rare and valuable that had been found in the tomb of a pharaoh or famous king.

"It looks like a little moon to me," Richie said sleepily, who obviously didn't have images of a dead king's trea-

33

sure in his mind. "I think you were right after all, David. This is the best place ever."

David listened as Richie began to snuffle in his sleep. Maybe the best, maybe not. But we're still together, he reminded himself. That's what counts. Still together. Not Richie one place, and me somewhere else.

Chapter Six

When the principal, Mr. Bateman, walked into room 103, David's heart leapfrogged from his chest into his throat. The principal of any school was a They. Theys were in charge of what happened to you, just like Child Aid workers.

He began to feel slightly damp around the back of his neck. Although the room was cool, he realized he was sweating under the waistband of his jeans too. The sensation was familiar: He was scared, and his bowels responded, as they always did, by contorting themselves into knots.

Mr. Bateman conferred with Mrs. Olson near the door. They turned their shoulders toward the pencil sharpener to shield their words, heads together, and spoke in hushed voices.

With Mrs. Olson's attention diverted, a lively beehive hum quickly filled the room. In the front row, Linda Lundy began to comb her long yellow hair. Mark French pitched a spitball across the room to Daryl Remax. Evil Evan Ellis stuck his foot across the aisle and rammed it under David's desk as if he had a right to that space along with what he could legally claim beneath his own. David pretended not to notice.

Mr. Bateman nodded a final time, then stepped outside. From the front of the room Mrs. Olson called out, in tones that weren't as brightly colored as usual, "David? Could you come up here a moment, please?"

Oh, jeez. David tried to remember if he hadn't put his stuff in the right places in the lunchroom. Maybe that was the problem. Paper went in the barrel, plates and cups in the blue plastic bin, silverware on the tray. Maybe he'd gotten them mixed up. Maybe one of his forks had jammed up the dish-washing machine. A repairperson had been called; it would cost the school a ton of money; and now . . .

Mrs. Olson clasped his wrist lightly and drew him closer to her desk. "David, Mr. Bateman is waiting for you outside. There's been . . . um . . . an accident."

She must have seen alarm blossom on his face because she added quickly, "I'm sure Richie's fine, David. Just the same, they've taken him to Miller Memorial. You know, to be on the safe side. Mr. Bateman thought it best if you could be with him, Richie being only in third grade and all."

"What . . . happened?" David heard himself ask. A car—had one hit Richie? Had he gone into the street at recess? The littler kids had recess at a different time; he hadn't been there to personally look after the little goofball. David could plainly see his brother lying broken and bleeding against the curb, his glasses smashed, his eyes closed.

"No, no, nothing like that," Mrs. Olson assured him. Her fingers on his wrist were warm and fluttery. "It happened during lunch. According to what Mr. Bateman told me a moment ago, apparently something didn't settle well in Richie's tummy. He isn't sure if it was the pizza or what. Your brother had quite a reaction, and the school nurse thought it best if he went straight to the emergency room."

People went to emergency rooms because of pizza? David felt himself sigh with relief, but didn't actually hear himself make any noise. It couldn't be very serious. Richie had always really liked pizza. If it'd been a problem for him, he'd have known about it way before now.

"Now don't worry, David," Mrs. Olson murmured, then urged him toward the door. "Mr. Bateman is waiting for you, dear, so you're excused from class now." Her smile was sympathetic.

Outside, Mr. Bateman laid a comradely hand on his shoulder. "I'm sure you're one of the first people that Richie will want to see," he said. His voice was as mild and amiable as Evan Ellis's. "My car's right out here. Why don't I just run you over to Miller Memorial right now?"

When Mr. Bateman pulled up at the emergency entrance, David thought he saw a gray car just like Mrs. Birk's parked nearby. Inside, he discovered that indeed it was hers. Her smile was a lot like Mrs. Olson's, and she patted the space beside her on a sofa in the waiting room. When David sat down, she fussed with his collar and smoothed his hair.

"It's going to be fine, David," she assured him. "I'm sure there's really nothing at all to worry about. But as soon as Mr. Bateman called me, I decided I ought to be here with you. And Richie too, of course."

David was still amazed at the fuss created by some pizza. Richie had probably eaten too much. Or too fast. He could be a real pig sometimes.

The doctor who came through a pair of swinging doors at the end of the hall was short and had the pinkest face David had ever seen. It was round and shiny, made all the cheerier by a pair of small eyes the color of a robin's egg.

He smiled agreeably, and sat down on a straight-backed chair opposite the couch. He placed his hands on his knees. His fingers were short and plump and also very pink. They reminded David of the paws of a possum he'd seen once along the railroad track that he and Richie used to walk along to visit Gramma at the Day's End Senior Center.

"Are you the young man's brother?" the doctor asked. His voice was gentle and pleasing to listen to.

David nodded. "Yes, sir. Richie's younger than me. He's in third grade."

"Ah." The doctor seemed not to know exactly what to say next. He studied his possum paws. "These are always difficult moments," he confessed.

"What was there about the pizza that upset Richie so badly?" Mrs. Birk inquired, as if to help the doctor get started again.

"Ah, the pizza," the doctor said. "It wasn't the pizza, exactly, but a certain food additive that might have been in the sauce or perhaps the meat. We'll have it analyzed so we can pinpoint the problem. Some people are extremely allergic to such additives, you see." He tapped his knees with his short, pink possum fingers. "The truth, I regret to have to tell you, is that I'm afraid we've lost Richie."

David frowned. Suddenly, he felt a little angry.

What? They'd lost Richie? Had they just brought him here after he got sick on Franklin Elementary's stupid lousy school lunch and then turned him loose in the halls, expecting him to hold his own head over some toilet and upchuck all by himself? Some hospital.

If Richie was still wandering around, why, he'd be getting scareder and scareder. Every time he turned a corner and saw that everything looked strange and white and silent, and smelled that peculiar, clean smell that a hospital always had, he'd feel so . . .

David got up and moved toward the swinging doors. "We better start to look for him right away," he suggested.

The doctor pressed him gently back onto the sofa cushions. "Let me try to tell you what seems to have happened, David," he said. David concentrated, and listened carefully to the explanation.

"Your brother—as you probably know better than anyone else, David—had an allergic condition. Almost always, such a condition can be successfully controlled by ordinary medication."

Condition. Controlled. Medication. Yes, David agreed silently, that was true. Richie did have allergies, and he used an inhaler sometimes. Lately, though, he hadn't been bothered much. So far, even beady-eyed hairy old Wendell hadn't caused him any special grief.

"Once in a while—and I want to emphasize that it's a very rare, highly unusual occurrence—a person such as Richie, who over a period of time has become extremely sensitized to a variety of allergens, can experience what we call an anaphylactic reaction."

A rare occurrence. Richie had just had some kind of

an experience. Anna-fa-lack-tick. It sounded like a girl's name, sort of. Anna Falacktick. Maybe she came from a foreign country, and hardly spoke English at all. Maybe she was a person like Evil Evan Ellis—bigger than Richie, and maybe she'd held him down in the lunchroom and stuffed his mouth full of pizza even after he'd gotten mad at her and yelled, "No, I don't want any more!"

"There are drugs that can be administered to persons who suffer such life-threatening reactions, and if they are given quickly, usually there are no long-term consequences," the doctor went on.

Administered. Life-threatening. No consequences. David waited.

"In Richie's case, however, his reaction to the additive in the pizza was sudden and extremely serious. The outcome might not have been changed even if an ambulance had been called. You see, in the very brief time that it took Mr. Bateman to bring Richie to our emergency room, your brother's medical situation became irreversible." The doctor patted his own knees again. "Richie's condition became . . . ah . . . fatal."

"Irreversible?" David echoed. "Fatal?"

The doctor seemed to have used all the words he had saved up. He sat back, and David noticed that his smile had faded. His cheery blue eyes were filled with sorrow.

At his side, David sensed Mrs. Birk lean forward and felt her warm hand cover his own. Across the room, the light angled off the gold rims of Mr. Bateman's glasses with blinding brightness.

"David, I believe the doctor means that Richie died," Mrs. Birk said gently. Her voice seemed to come from the bottom of a deep well.

David turned to look at her. The sun had welded each of her corkscrew curls into a sturdy silver helmet such as astronauts wear. The expression in her eyes was tender, like the doctor's.

No. Of course it couldn't be. There'd been a terrible mistake. Why, he'd promised Richie himself that they'd never be separated, and they never had been. No, not ever. Not once. David looked around for something familiar to fix his eyes on. For a glimpse of Richie.

The swinging doors at the end of the room didn't swing open. Richie didn't peek around the corner of one of them and cry, "Fooled ya!"

"Richie?" David called out loud. "Don't be scared, Richie. Just say something to let me know where you are. I'll come to find you, Richie, just like when you got lost that time in the SuperValu, remember? It'll be okay, Richie. Just like always. Richie?"

The room was silent. Outside, in a pool of pale spring sunshine on the window ledge, David saw three pigeons. One of them had a breast of iridescent blue-green feathers. The pigeons nodded and curtsied to one another. Their voices were muffled and polite beyond the glass.

Oh, Richie! I told you this would be the best place ever. You believed what I said. I believed it, too. David's heart was as still and cold as a stone in his chest. *Oh, Richie!*

Chapter Seven

"It's time to go now, David," Mrs. Birk called from the bottom of the stairs.

David stayed where he was, hunched cross-legged in the middle of Richie's bed. Richie always had a certain smell about him. Partly sweet, partly sour, and his bed-clothes still smelled that way. David sniffed. He breathed deeply again. That smell made Richie seem not gone.

"David? Are you ready to go? Mr. Birk has started the car. We don't want to be late this afternoon, now do we, dear?" Her question was the wheedling, please-be-a-good-boy kind. David didn't budge.

A moment later, he heard footfalls coming up the stairs, down the hall, across the room. Mrs. Birk perched on the bed opposite him. She balanced her lumpy black purse on her knees.

"Oh, David," she sighed. "I know how hard this must be for you."

"No you don't," he said. "You never had a brother who died from pizza." The black handbag on her knees looked wicked. "How can you if you never had a brother in third grade who died from a lousy school lunch?"

Mrs. Birk sighed again. She didn't seem to have an answer. "You'll always regret it if you don't come with us today," she said finally.

"No I won't."

"Your parents have been notified, David. If your mother is up to it, she'll most likely be at the funeral. Your daddy too. They'll want to see you, I'm sure."

"Who cares?"

"You do, David. Deep down, dear, I know you do."

"Don't call me dear. Anyway, they never took care of me and Richie when we were alive."

What had he said? That both he and Richie were dead? Well, it was true. He was just as dead as Richie would ever be.

The urgent sound of the car motor as Mr. Birk tapped the accelerator floated up from the driveway. "Mr. Birk and I will have to leave in a couple of minutes, David," Mrs. Birk murmured. She hesitated a moment longer.

"Are you sure you want to stay here all by yourself?" Suddenly, she brightened. "Of course, Wendell's here and he'd be happy to keep you company. Why don't I ask him to come upstairs right now? He can stay with you while—"

"Forget Wendell!" David said loudly. He had always tried to be nice with fosters, hadn't he? He never broke windows, never asked for seconds, never peed in his bed, and always made sure Richie didn't do any of those things either. So where had it gotten him? Nowhere. In spite of everything, Richie was gone. David vowed he'd never be nice to anyone again.

"I don't want stupid old Wendell to keep me company!" he yelled. "I don't want to see anybody! Go to the dumb old funeral by yourself!"

Mrs. Birk patted his knee, and David flinched. He didn't want Wendell's company—or for anyone to pat him. Most especially, he didn't want to hear any minister in any church says things about Richie. Or go to any cemetery where there'd be flowers and the sound of birds singing from bare tree branches and strangers who whispered while the sun gleamed on the snow-covered grass.

Anyway, they weren't burying Richie. Richie was— well, he was somewhere else. No way was Richie in a coffin, his eyes closed behind glasses someone had polished until the lenses were finally clean. No way would they stick the real Richie in the ground in a hole as black and cunning as Mrs. Birk's ugly purse.

Mrs. Birk retreated down the stairs and closed the front door behind her. A moment later, David heard the car leave the driveway, move slowly down the street, turn the corner.

He went to the window and stared down into the backyard.

Only a few days ago he and Richie had finished building the bridge over a ravine they'd made after brushing snow off the sand. In a moment, while the Birks were gone to the funeral, he'd go out there and wreck it. The racetrack and all the mountains too. He'd smash everything. He'd never build bridges or mountains or racetracks ever again. The one-eyed bear leaning against the window casement seemed to offer sympathy. David stared hard at him. "Dumb, stupid bear!" he hollered. He picked it up, threw it across the room. The bear hit the wall, skittered across the floor into the hallway, and his other eye popped out. David heard it go clicking down the stairs. Fine. Now the bear was blind. Now he couldn't see that Richie was gone.

He looked at the other treasures Richie liked so well. One by one, David took them from the windowsill and dropped them into the wooden box with the rope handle. He pitched Richie's new yellow notebook in. He grabbed the bear by one leg and threw him in too. When Mr. Hutton came to take him to a new foster home—it was only a matter of time till he did—David vowed not to take anything with him. No way would he haul Richie's treasures from place to place anymore.

David flopped onto Richie's bed and pressed his face into the pillow. He sniffed deeply of Richie's partly sweet, partly sour smell. He curled up and kept his face pressed into the pillow. He wondered if he would cry. He didn't.

"You don't have to go to school today if you don't feel like it," Mrs. Birk said kindly on Monday morning. "Mr. Bateman told me that he'd let me bring your homework to you and carry your lessons back to school until you feel better."

"I'm not sick. I feel fine," David said. In a weird way, he did. There was a cold, solid column in his middle that stretched from just above his collarbone to past his belly button. It made him feel cool and strong all over. With that column to hold him up, everything seemed ordinary and unexceptional. He didn't even feel lonely.

This morning, he prayed that Evil Evan Ellis would be waiting on the corner. It would be perfect if Evil would grab him, throw him to the ground, jump on his back, and kick him all over with his heavy shoes.

David could feel the blows rain against his ribs, felt blood spurt from his nose, welcomed the sensation of his eyes swelling shut from the terrible beating Evan would give him. He relished the pain that was soon to come. If Evil Evan didn't haul off and smash him good, David decided he'd hit Evan first.

Ah. There he was, on the corner as usual. His cronies were with him.

David marched forward, eager to be bashed and smashed and broken to bits, then left on the sidewalk, bleeding heavily and too injured to be moved to a hospital. He would look silently up at the faces bending over him. "I'm dying," he'd whisper. And then he would.

When he came abreast of the threesome on the corner, they stepped respectfully aside. "Sorry about your brother," Evil Evan offered gently. "Tough go, man."

David stared. "What's wrong with you?" he heard himself screech. "'Tough go'—what's that s'posed to mean? Know something, Ellis? You're an—an—idiot! A jackass! A butthead!"

The words were intoxicating. David tried to think of other horrible words that would drive Evan into a murderous rage but those were the only three he could think of so he said them all again.

"Idiot! Jackass! Butthead!" he shrieked. Evil didn't look murderous, though—merely mournful. Enraged, David flew to school, the cool column in his middle melting out through his toes, his knees weakening.

In class, Mrs. Olson's voice of primary colors had faded to pale lavender, pink, and peach. "It's nice to see you, David," she said. "How are you feeling?"

"Fine!" he yelled. "Why does everyone think I been sick or something? My brother died. That's all. Big deal. He was a pain in the neck, anyway. He smelled weird and his glasses were always dirty and he expected me to be a mom and a dad to him all the time."

David waited for Mrs. Olson give him detention or tell him to report to Mr. Bateman's office at once but she didn't do either one. Instead, her hand on his shoulder was motherly and helpful. That touch felt horrible, so he jerked away, careened down the aisle, and hurled himself into his seat.

"Just forget it, okay? Forget it!"

In the front row, Linda Lundy quit combing her long yellow hair and turned to give him a sad little smile. Her blue eyes were shiny, as if tears of sympathy were about to spill down her smooth, pale cheeks.

David stuck his tongue out at her, put his thumbs in his ears, waggled his fingers furiously at her. He was glad when she turned red and started to comb her hair again, this time so hard and fast that it got electrified and stuck out all around her head like a huge yellow bush. Dumb, stupid Linda Lundy! Dumb, stupid world!

In the middle of the week, Mrs. Birk gave him a present. Three goldfish in a bowl. She gave him a box of food, and showed him how to feed them. At night, though, David could hear the fish rise to the surface of the water and slurp. The sound was melancholy and depressing.

He got out of bed and draped his jacket over the bowl. Ignorant, stupid fish. He ought to flush them down the toilet. Tomorrow, maybe he would.

* * *

47

At the end of the week, Mrs. Birk made an announcement. "I think I have some good news for you, David," she began.

First fish. Now she had good news. David decided he'd changed his mind about her. As foster mothers went, she was as awful as any of them. Some ignored you, which right now would've been a relief. Some cared too much, like Mrs. Birk.

In all the world, there could be no good news, because the only news that would mean anything would be if someone—who would have such power, David couldn't imagine—would say that Richie's death had been a mistake. That God was going to send him back, that his name had been accidentally called up due to a glitch in a heavenly computer. Richie wasn't dead after all, someone would report in a deep voice, and Mr. Hutton had been instructed to bring him back in the morning.

Mrs. Birk's news wasn't anything like that.

"Mr. Hutton called and told me that everyone at the Child Aid Department thinks it best for you to continue to stay with Mr. Birk and me," she said, smiling. "It means you won't have to move again, or at least not for a while."

David knew she was looking at him expectantly, as if the news would cheer him up. He kept his eyes on his plate.

Since Richie was gone, food didn't taste right anymore. Before, he'd liked Mrs. Birk's meatballs and gravy; now they reminded him of dog doo slathered with thick brown axle grease.

"And that's not the only news I have," Mrs. Birk continued. David sensed that she glanced at Mr. Birk as if to say, Surely *this* will cheer him up. "I asked Mr. Hutton to please bring us another foster child."

David looked up. "Nobody can take Richie's place," he warned.

He thought about Richie's empty bed. He wanted it to stay empty. If they put anyone else in it, it would be as if Richie hadn't mattered, that one kid was the same as any other kid, that one could be exchanged for another and it didn't make any difference at all.

"I plan to put the newcomer across the hall," Mrs. Birk agreed, as if she understood exactly what he was thinking. "I realize that you need your privacy." Her voice was kind, but that sort of kindness made David feel as if he might cry.

He swallowed hard. "Can I go upstairs now?" he croaked. "I don't feel so good."

"Of course, David," Mrs. Birk said. "Later, maybe you'd like to take Wendell for a walk." Hearing his name, Wendell raised his ears. His sweet, beady eyes were hopeful.

"I'm not going to feel better that quick," David warned. It gave him a wicked satisfaction to see that Wendell dropped his ears. Wendell had no right to be happy. Nobody did. Richie was gone. Without Richie, the world had a big hole in it that no one, not even God, could glue a patch over.

Chapter Eight

Two weeks later, the Child Aid worker's car was at the curb when David got home from school.

He tiptoed around to the back door and was careful not to make crunchy sounds in the lingering piles of snow beside the steps. No way did he want to see anyone now, least of all Mr. Hutton or the new kid who was being delivered to Mrs. Birk.

He would put off meeting whoever it was for as long as possible. Instead, he'd sneak into the kitchen, then go quietly straight upstairs. Later, he'd say he felt too sick to come down for supper. In the morning, he wouldn't get out of bed either. Let that new kid hoof it to school alone.

Mrs. Birk saw him, though, and called out. Her voice was full of those same glowing red, yellow, and blue colors that Mrs. Olson's had been on the first day of school. "Come meet our new guest, David," she invited.

David moved as slowly as a turtle toward the archway that led into the living room. Why'd they have to get a new kid so soon? he asked himself. Couldn't everyone have waited a couple of months, at least?

Such a short time had passed since Richie was . . . um . . . ah . . . buried.

He eased himself around the side of the archway without lifting his feet off the floor. There was Mr. Hutton on the sofa, thin and pale as ever, frowning down the length of his long pickle nose. Mrs. Birk was in her favorite chair across from the TV. Wendell sat at her feet and smiled expectantly at the newcomer.

David stared, unable to believe what he saw next to the front door, looking like a prisoner hoping for a way to escape from jail.

Not only was she ugly, she was a girl.

From her looks, she had to be older than he was by at least a year. Her legs were so skinny that David didn't see how they could hold her up. Her knees were rusty from not being washed too often. She was poised on the balls of her feet as if at any moment she intended to fling open the door and fly off down the street.

He held his breath, and hoped she would.

"This is Olivia," Mrs. Birk announced.

"Ollie!" the girl hollered in a voice that seemed to fill the room with boiling oil to within an inch of the ceiling. Her eyes, which were the same queer, pale color as certain lemon-lime sodas, glowed so hotly that David wondered if her glance might set fire to everything she looked at. Furniture, drapes, carpet. Him.

He could see right away that this Ollie person had never been afraid like he and Richie always were. She obviously was not a girl who'd ever worried a whit about breaking windows or wetting her bed.

She raked her dirty fingers through her hair, which was short, frizzy, and orange. "Ollie!" she yelled again.

"You just better call me Ollie because it fits me a lot better than dumb O-liv-ee-ya!"

David shuddered. And Mrs. Birk had thought it would be good news that he wouldn't be moved for a while? He wished he could walk out right now, climb into Mr. Hutton's car, and be taken away this very instant.

After supper (during which Ollie criticized the food and threw mean looks at Wendell), David heard the newcomer rattling around in her room. It sounded almost as if she was moving furniture. When he peeked around his door, he saw that was exactly what she was doing.

"What you staring at?" she demanded. Her lemon-lime gaze was as deadly as battery acid. "You never seen anybody change a room around before?"

David didn't answer.

"I don't like to be sneaked up on after the lights are out," she snapped. "Understand? I'll lock this here door tonight by shoving this dresser in front of it. So if you got any smart ideas, buster, just forget 'em."

David wondered if he should explain that most certainly he would never have a smart idea that involved her, of all people, but he was sure Ollie wouldn't have paid any attention if he tried. She was fiercely intent upon what she was doing, and made such a racket that finally Mrs. Birk came up the stairs to find out what was going on.

"Whatever in the world—?" she began.

"Don't like to be sneaked up on in the dark," Ollie barked. She glared at Mrs. Birk with her glittery, battery-acid eyes. "A person has to take care of herself," she added, as if that explained everything.

"Yes, dear, I think I understand what you mean," Mrs. Birk agreed. "Later, after you've been with us awhile, you might feel differently."

"No I won't," Ollie declared firmly. "I been a foster too long. I know the system inside and out. I've learned too much. A person's gotta be careful. All the time." Mrs. Birk patted Ollie's shoulder, but the girl jumped away as if the touch was hot.

"Good-night!" she yelled, and slammed her door shut.

Standing in the hall beside Mrs. Birk, David heard the sound of the dresser being hauled in front of the door on the other side.

"It worries me a little," Mrs. Birk whispered.

David nodded. "She could scratch up the floor pretty bad," he whispered back.

"It's not that, dear. But what if the house were to catch on fire? How would we get her out?"

"I'd jump out the window!" came a screech from behind the closed door. "You think I'm dumb, or what?"

David turned to Mrs. Birk, and was surprised to see her smile. She shrugged lightly, put a finger to her lips, then tiptoed back down the stairs.

David waited alone in the hallway. "What're you standing there for?" came a second screech. "Get over there into your own room where you belong!"

David crept into his room as Ollie ordered. For a long time he sat on his bed. It would be nice if there was some way he could tell Richie what was going on.

Maybe he'd try, even though Richie was far away and might not be able to hear.

Listen, Richie, you won't believe what's happening. The Birks, well, they got this new foster kid. She's a girl.

She's got eyes the color of Gatorade, and her knees are so dirty that even Mrs. Birk'll never get 'em clean. She's older than either me or you, and she's got a voice as soft and smooth as a tubful of broken glass. Her name's Ollie, and I don't think she's ever been afraid.

David waited. Richie's dear, sweet-sour smell was beginning to fade from his pillow, his bedspread, the room.

David hugged himself. Oh, Richie! Come back, Richie! he called silently. Come back!

Chapter Nine

Mrs. Birk had preregistered Ollie and had gotten all her supplies, which meant that the very next morning Ollie was ready to start school. Hurrying two steps behind her as she strode down the street in front of him, David realized he wouldn't be the new kid anymore.

He was surprised that fact didn't bring him more relief than it did.

The truth was, even though Ollie was tall and homely and had a voice that could peel paint off walls, he didn't relish the notion of what she'd have to endure on her first day at Franklin Elementary.

It might be a good idea to warn her about Evil Evan Ellis, David decided. He cleared his throat.

"What's wrong with you?" Ollie snapped. No matter what she said, her voice always sounded more like you thought a boy's should sound than a girl's. There was something boyish in her walk, too. She leaned forward, knees bent slightly, as if she were pressing into a strong head wind along a deserted beach near some ocean. David cleared his throat again.

"That's the third time you've done that! Some frog

take up residence next to your windpipe, or what? Nothing drives me crazier than people who are *nervous.*" She made the word sound like a terrible disease that a person ought to get treatment for as quickly as possible.

"There's this kid," David said.

"What kid?"

"You know—the kind who makes trouble."

"Shoot! There's that kind of kid everywhere you go," Ollie scoffed. "You could go to the moon, and guess what you'd find up there? Behind some moon rock or a scrubby little old moon tree you'd find a kid who makes trouble. So what else is new?"

"Yeah, but I wanted to warn you," David persisted. "So you wouldn't be surprised. This guy didn't bother Richie much, but one day he bent my arm up between my shoulder blades till I thought he'd bust it for sure."

Ollie's bright, frizzy hair stuck straight out over her forehead, like the bill of a baseball cap. Her profile was as sharp and clean as a blade in the morning air, and a grim smile turned up a corner of her mouth. She hiked her shoulders as if the threat of getting *her* arm cranked up between her shoulder blades was a challenge she positively looked forward to.

"So who's this Richie?" she demanded. Her pale eyes were narrow, and David realized his answer was only of passing significance to her because she was already savoring her encounter with Evil Evan Ellis.

"Richie was . . ." David paused. *Was.*

How could he speak of Richie in the past tense? But if he said *is* that wouldn't be right either, because Richie wasn't actually here, walking to school between him and Ollie this morning. Richie was . . . somewhere else.

Not buried. Not dead. Just . . . elsewhere. David had decided he didn't believe much in heaven anymore, but of course Richie couldn't be in hell, so he must be . . . well, just someplace else.

"Well?" Ollie barked. "There some big secret about this Richie kid?"

"Richie . . . died." It was a word like fate. Solid, blocky, unmovable.

"Died?" Instantly, Ollie was interested. "He someone you knew? The Child Aid folks send you two guys to the Birks at the same time?"

"Richie and me are . . . ah, we were . . . brothers."

Ollie was silent. Her footfalls on the sidewalk, which a moment before had sounded as if she weighed two hundred pounds, became light and discreet.

"Hey, listen. I'm sorry, kid. Bad luck happens, y'know? When'd he die?" She said the word easily, as if it were no special stranger to her.

"Three weeks ago."

"Ummm. That's not very long." She sighed. "Funerals can be hard. I been to a few myself, so I know. My aunt died, and I went to hers. The church ladies served lemonade and teeny-weeny sandwiches in the church basement. Then my grampa died, and I went to his. No sandwiches that time, though."

David was silent. "I didn't go to Richie's," he admitted.

Ollie whirled in front of him, blocked his way on the sidewalk, and stared him down with her bony fists rammed against her bony hips.

"You never went to your own brother's funeral?" Her narrow face was hard with disbelief. "If I had a brother—a sister even, and even if she was a person I

hated because she was beautifuller than a princess—
why, if that person died, I'd for sure go to their funeral.
You bet I would." Her pale-green stare judged him
harshly, accusing him of being a bad brother.

David didn't answer. He only shook his head. He
didn't even want to think about that day. About Mrs.
Birk's cunning black purse. About any of that. Ollie
moved aside, then fell into step beside him again, no
longer marching along so fast that he had to almost run
to keep up with her. But before he could sort out the
words to explain why he'd never gone to the funeral or
to the cemetery, David spied Evan Ellis on the corner
with his buddies.

"That's him," he said, nodding his head in the direction of the threesome on the corner. He decided it
wouldn't be smart to point.

"The tall guy? He the dude that gives you grief?"
David nodded again, not wishing to look too long or
too hard at the trio.

"Listen, buster, I been in the system a long time,"
Ollie reminded David, her words as edged and dangerous as knives. "One thing you learn after you been a
foster as long as I been. It's my motto: Don't Take Crap.
That's my motto all right. No crap. Not from anybody.
Not even once. It solves a lot of problems before they
even get started."

As they approached Evil Evan and his cronies, David
heard snickers.

"Dippy dorky David got himself a bodyguard!"

"Hey—ain't that RoboWoman?"

"Looka that hair! What circus they let her out of?"

Ollie stopped dead in her tracks. The group fell unex-
pectedly silent under her scalding, pea-green gaze.

"Somebody say something?" she demanded. Nobody answered, though the snickers began again as soon as she looked away.

"RoboWoman!" Robbie Williams croaked.

"Dippy dorky David got a bodyguard!" Jim Ellman snorted.

"Just got outa the circus!" they chimed together.

Evan Ellis didn't say a word. He stepped into the middle of the sidewalk and stood there, legs braced wide apart. "Careful, you'll be late for school," he purred in his tender, soft-hard voice. "Sure be too bad if you guys got detention for being tardy, now wouldn't it?"

He smirked, and reached out to tug on Ollie's short, stiff, bright bangs. "Shoosh! Talk about a dumb-looking babe!"

David didn't actually see Ollie wind up her fist. It just seemed as if suddenly it was out there in the air. Not a girl-sized fist either, but one that was knotted and hard as a boxer's. She *ka-powed* Evan Ellis square in the middle of his smiling face. His head snapped back, and it was only an instant before he looked as if he'd been splattered with catsup.

"Back off, buster," Ollie warned, her words as cold and square as ice cubes. "You don't give me trouble, I don't give you none. Got it?"

Evan crouched over his knees, and cupped his damaged nose in both hands. The noise that floated up sounded sort of like "Eeeooouuuwww!" Catsup leaked through his fingers onto the sidewalk.

Robbie Williams leaped onto the snow-crusted boulevard as if the sidewalk had mysteriously become too hot to stand on.

59

Jim Ellman stood sideways, as if he didn't even know the other two and had only been hurrying past on his way to somewhere else.

Ollie marched toward Franklin Elementary at a brisk, military pace. "Oh, shoot!" she groaned. "There's gonna be a ton of trouble over this. You just wait, there will." She sighed heavily. "Always is. Only thing, it's worse if you take crap. Take my advice, kid. No crap."

David hurried along beside her, then sneaked a quick peek at her. It was as if she regretted having to do what she'd done, that it was something she'd had to do lots of times before. Apparently, it never got any easier.

Chapter Ten

David pretended that he wasn't really waiting for anyone. He offered to clean the blackboards for Mrs. Olson. The big kids in sixth got out thirty minutes later than the kids from the lower grades, so if he happened to run into Ollie as she came down the hall, such a meeting would seem like an accident.

"Mr. Brown will come by to do that later, David," Mrs. Olson murmured as soon as he began to clean the blackboards. David finished them all anyway. Then he decided he'd better clean Harry the Hamster's cage. Daryl Remax had brought Harry for show-and-tell. The rest of the class weren't impressed because they said they had their own hamsters or guinea pigs at home, but David was pleased by everything about Harry—his cheerful little eyes especially.

"Daryl really ought to do that himself," Mrs. Olson pointed out. Harry's bedding was changed, his water freshened, and pellets put in his feeder, and even though Mrs. Olson didn't seem particularly eager for any assistance in putting away the paper supplies, David helped with that too.

Next, he straightened out his desk, which, in only five weeks, hadn't had time to get especially messy. It was almost three-thirty before Mrs. Olson was ready to lock the door.

David took a long drink at the fountain at the end of the hall. The three-thirty bell rang, and around the corner he could hear kids thunder out of their rooms in the other wing. He leaned over to take another drink as they roared past, and kept an eye peeled for Ollie.

Nowhere could she be seen bobbing along on the river of sixth graders that flowed by. David waited till the hall was empty. He scraped his heels on the floor and felt queerly pleased to see that he left black scuff marks for Mr. Brown to clean up. Maybe he should go down to the sixth-grade rooms and see if Ollie had been kept after school.

Both of the rooms at the end of the other wing were already locked and dark. David felt the knot in his belly tighten as he realized what had probably happened.

Ollie had already been expelled.

Mr. Hutton had been called to come and get her. He probably hadn't even let her go back to Mrs. Birk's to pack her stuff before he carted her away to a different foster home. David knew what Theys called kids like Ollie. Incorrigible. Once Theys called you that, you were done for.

David walked slowly into the nearly deserted school yard. A light breeze moved the swings where two second graders were playing. Richie had liked those swings, too. David kicked at the gravel as he crossed the playground.

The second graders fell silent as he passed, but David heard one of them whisper, "That's him. He's the one with the brother that died. From school lunch." The words were reverent and full of respect.

Then he saw Ollie. She was leaning against the back side of the school, a knee bent, resting one foot against the building. She was smoking.

Smoking!

"You're not supposed to do that," David warned her.

"Lean against their dumb school?" Ollie sneered. "You crazy or what? You think it's a leaning tower of pizza or something? 'Fraid I might tip the dumb stupid thing over?" She pressed her back flatter against the building as if to test it, and gave him a bitter smile.

"Smoke. You're not supposed to smoke."

"So make me stop, you little creep." She inhaled deeply, then dropped the cigarette stub to the ground and expertly mashed it into the gravel with the toe of her sneaker.

"I tried to quit," she admitted. "I was doing okay too, hadn't had one in a whole week, but that crap this morning really stressed me out. My nerves needed a smoke." She gave him a hard look. "'Course you wouldn't know about that."

David leaned against the building himself and wished he could tell her what he knew about nerves that were stretched too thin and bowels that tied themselves in knots. "I went down to your room and you weren't there," he said instead. "I figured they'd expelled you already."

"How'd you know which room I was in?"

"There's only two sixth grades. Figured you had to be in one of 'em."

Ollie pushed herself away from the building and strode off toward the Birks'. She pulled her arms out of the sleeves of her jacket and hugged herself as the empty tubes swung at her sides. Her orange hair jutted over her forehead and she squinted against the glare of the afternoon sun.

"So are they going to expel you?" David asked, and hoped she wouldn't think he was being too nosy.

"Nope. Worse'n that." Ollie sucked on her lower lip and scowled.

David couldn't imagine what could be worse. They walked in silence for half a block.

"I have to start going to these special classes every Friday," Ollie said finally. Her voice was low, and she hitched her shoulders up around her ears.

"What classes?" He suspected that too many questions would irritate her as much as throat clearing did, and regretted having to ask another one. She walked faster, and soon he was almost galloping to stay even.

"It's about attitudes and stuff. They got this plan to change my attitude. Help me see things in a different light, Mr. Bateman said. Light, schmight."

"What's this class called?"

Ollie stopped dead at the corner and whirled on him like a caged animal that has been poked at too often with a sharp stick.

"Is it just your basic nature to be dumber than a post?" she demanded. "That all you do—ask questions? Follow people home from school and bug 'em till they lose their minds? Don't you have anything more constructive to do with your time? Get a paper route or something!"

She rammed her arms back into the sleeves of her jacket. "Dumb class is called Conflict Negotiation," she grumbled. "You ever hear of anything so idiotic? Conflict nee-go-she-a-shun." She sneered over each syllable. "Big, hairy deal." She crossed the street at a lope, and David stepped up his pace beside her.

"What . . . do . . . they . . . teach you?" he panted.

"You hafta sit down and talk about stuff. Why you hit people. Why you get ticked off all the time. You're supposed to *talk* about whacking folks instead of actually hauling off and doing it, I guess. Makes no sense to me whatsoever. Let's face it, it sure doesn't fit my motto too well."

"Maybe it'll turn out to be a good class," David suggested hopefully.

Ollie snorted. "It might—if I was in it all alone. I'm gonna have company, though."

"Other kids? Like from other schools? They plan to get all you incorrigibles together and then try to teach—"

"No, dumbhead. I mean from Franklin. I mean your dear old buddy, Evan Ellis. Him and me got to go to this class together." Ollie pasted a sick-silly look on her face, and her voice rose an octave, making it sound more like a girl's. "We gotta learn how to 'resolve our differences civilly,'" she said, using the words David figured Mr. Bateman had already used on her and Evan.

David imagined Evil and Ollie seated across a table in Mr. Bateman's office, eyeballing each other. In the vision that popped into his head, Ollie's glare was the color of warm pee and Evan was holding his nose, his fingers still leaking catsup. He smiled.

"What's there to grin about?" Ollie yelled. From her glance, David realized she was mad enough to clobber him just like she'd clobbered Evan Ellis.

David wiped the smile off his face. "I think it's a good idea," he said. He meant it too. "I'd like to learn about con-flict nee-go-she-a-shun myself. When you're done, maybe you can teach me." If he could learn how to do it, the next time he had to go to a new school, maybe it wouldn't be such a hassle when he met a kid who had trouble written all over him.

At supper, Ollie ate like a person sentenced to a long term in solitary. Rushed; wordless; seeming not to taste her food. Without asking to be excused, she got up and clumped two at a time up the stairs to her room. Moments later everyone at the table could hear the grinding of the dresser being pulled into place in front of her door.

"I hate to think what that floor's going to look like when that girl leaves," Mr. Birk said, shaking his head while Wendell studied the ceiling.

When that girl leaves. Well, that's what it was all about, wasn't it? David thought. When you were a foster, you hung around a place for only just so long, then were moved on. Which made him feel bad for himself, but tonight, for some reason, he felt worse for Ollie.

After he went upstairs, David brushed his teeth and got ready for bed. He draped his jacket over the gold-fish, who swam giddily in circles as he lowered it over them, their gleaming sides telegraphing gold-and-silver messages as the water darkened. He wondered if . . .

He laid his jacket on the end of Richie's empty bed and walked across the hall in his sock feet so that Ollie couldn't hear him coming. He rapped lightly. She didn't answer. He knocked again, just as lightly but more insistently.

"Ollie," he whispered. "I got something for you."

He heard loud footfalls on the other side of the door; then as she pulled the dresser aside, he ran back to get the fish. The water was still sloshing a little, and the fish were giddier than ever when she pulled the door open a crack.

"Here. These are for you."

Ollie opened the door a little wider and peered down into the bowl. "Fish. What do I need fish for?" She sounded ungrateful.

"They're good pets. Real quiet." Too noisy for him, but David didn't mention that. "They won't claw your bedspread or make doo-doo on the floor." He held the bowl out to her. "Take 'em." He pressed the bowl into her hands.

"Well." Ollie's breath came out in a funny, surprised little puff. "That's nice of you. You sure you don't want to keep 'em yourself?"

"Yeah." He reached into his pocket for the box of fish food. "Just make sure you feed 'em twice a day. Not too much, though. And clean their bowl a couple of times a week. They're crazy for clean water. I guess it's got more oxygen in it and makes 'em feel real lively."

"What d'you call 'em?"

"Didn't name 'em." He hadn't wanted to. If he didn't give them names he wouldn't have to be glad Mrs. Birk had presented the fish to him in the first place.

Ollie peered into the bowl again. "Freddie . . . Frank . . . and Flo. That's what I'll call 'em." She cradled the bowl against her stomach, and David saw gold-and-silver signals flash between her parted fingers.

"Maybe you're not such a bad kid," she said, as if the possibility had caught her unaware.

When she closed her door, David wondered if she'd insist on moving the dresser back into place. There was no sound on the other side as she found a place to set the bowl. Then, grindingly, he heard the dresser tugged back to perform sentry duty.

"Hey, David," she called from the safety of her cell. "Thanks." It was the first time she'd called him anything but dumbhead, creep, or twerp.

David wished he could tell Richie what had just happened. But why did he keep trying? Richie was so far away he'd never be able to hear.

I gave Ollie the fish, Richie, David began. If you'd been here, Richie, I wouldn't have minded those weird slurpy sounds at night, but with you gone they made me feel awful. The real reason I gave 'em to Ollie, though, was on account of I think she's a lonely person. She'd never admit it, but I think she is. The fish will be nice company. With them, maybe she won't need to smoke anymore. That's what I did, Richie. I wanted you to know.

But it was hopeless. There was no sense trying to tell Richie anything.

Chapter Eleven

"Don't wait for me today," Ollie ordered when they walked to school the following Friday morning. "No telling how long I'll have to stay after school. Anyway, I'll be in no mood for any of your stupid questions." She pressed forward into the wind, though none of the remaining leaves on any branch was lifted by a breeze.

David waited anyway. On Fridays, Mrs. Olson was sometimes a little cranky, being eager to get home after a whole week of school, so he didn't offer to clean the blackboards again or straighten his desk, which was already straighter than any boy's needed to be.

Outside, he waited near the swings. Because he was there, the two second graders from Wednesday didn't come near. Instead, they hung close to the building, pointing at him and whispering. He knew they'd probably never eat pizza again, ever.

The shadows were long across the playground when Ollie finally came out. Her face was dark with anger, and she fumbled in her jacket for a smoke. David knew she wouldn't find any, though, because Mrs. Birk had taken them out and put the package in the garbage.

Ollie turned her pockets inside out, then rapped her knuckles against her forehead.

Evan Ellis came out next. He didn't look angry; instead, he seemed surprised.

He stared after Ollie as she loped down the street. David watched him turn and walk slowly in the opposite direction, then, when he was sure Evan was gone, he ran to catch up with Ollie himself.

"Told you not to wait!" she snapped irritably. "So help me, you ask me one single stupid question and I'll kill you. You hear me?"

David wondered how she might murder him, and debated about reminding her that he'd given her three fish. He wondered if he should tell Mrs. Birk to look under Ollie's mattress tonight to see if she'd hidden a weapon there. He trotted slightly behind her, and hoped that by the time she'd eaten supper she wouldn't feel so deadly.

"The whole thing's a joke," she said in her peel-the-paint-off-the-wall voice. "If Mr. Hutton hauls me off tomorrow, it won't be a minute too soon. I don't need this kinda aggravation. Take my word for it, I don't."

David took her word for it, and said nothing. It was Ollie herself who couldn't seem to stop talking.

"They even got this workbook we hafta fill out before our session next week. Can you believe it? A *workbook*, as if this was a legitimate class, which any idiot knows it isn't."

David glanced at the stuff sticking out of her hip pocket.

"It's like homework, even. We actually have to turn it in!"

David decided that maybe it was safe to speak. "Evan have to turn his in, too?"

"Of course, stupid," Ollie groaned. "I mean, we're in this together, right?" She paused and seemed to reflect on something that surprised her. "I guess this isn't the first time for him either. I been in trouble a kazillion million times before—but I hear tell he's been pushing people around practically since he was in first grade."

She sniffed in a superior way. "I got good reasons for what *I* do, though. Evan Ellis doesn't."

"It sure wasn't me who squealed on him," David pointed out, just in case Evan might get the idea that part of the trouble he was in was because of that crank-the-arm-up-between-the-shoulder-blades episode a few weeks ago.

"Don't sweat it. It was teachers, I guess, who complained the most. The other kids were just like you—too darn chicken-livered to open their yaps."

"I didn't say anything because I didn't want to make it worse," David explained.

Ollie slowed down. "I think I'll call Mr. Hutton as soon as we get home," she said, squinting thoughtfully into the distance. "I'll tell him I can't take it here anymore. I'll tell him if he doesn't come to get me I'll hit the road." She smiled with grim satisfaction. "That'll bring him running quick enough. The folks at the aid department hate for you to run off on 'em. Guess they figure it makes 'em look bad."

David slowed down, too. *Don't go, Ollie,* he wished he had nerve enough to say. That queer, cool feeling (lately, it had been warming a little) returned to his middle again, chilled him from his collarbone to past his belly button. *Don't go.* But he didn't say a word.

After she helped Mrs. Birk with the dishes, Ollie sat down at the kitchen table. She did some spelling, then a few math problems. Sighing heavily, she finally pulled her new workbook out from beneath her pile of stuff on the table.

"If you need any help with that, just let me know," Mrs. Birk called helpfully from the living room.

Ollie rolled her eyes at the suggestion, and nibbled on the end of her pencil. David sat across the table and pretended he had homework to do, too. He kept his head bent low so that Ollie wouldn't think he was prying.

"'What is your first response when someone verbally abuses you?'" she read out loud. "Now what's that supposed to mean?" she demanded. David looked up from the assigned chapter in his social studies book, which he'd already read twice. The Egyptians had a special method of preserving dead people, and no one, even today, knew exactly what it was.

"I think it means, like, if someone says mean things to you, does it make you mad," he suggested. "Like, does it make you want to punch somebody out."

"*Of course* that's how it makes me feel!" Ollie ranted. "I don't like for people to get on my case about how I look or how I act. Makes me as mean as a scalded dog."

"But maybe—" David began, but didn't have a chance to finish because Ollie snapped her workbook shut with a loud *thonk*. There were things he wanted to tell her about what he thought he already knew about conflict negotiation, but she thundered up the stairs before he could get the right words framed in his mind. He had figured this might be a good time to tell her what he and Richie had agreed on. Don't ask for seconds, don't break any windows, don't make yellow spots on the mattress.

David waited to hear the sound of the dresser being pulled in front of her door. When he didn't, he started to worry and went upstairs himself.

Ollie hadn't closed her door yet or pulled the dresser across it. She wasn't even in her own room. She was perched on the edge of Richie's bed, her hands clasped between her knees.

She bounced lightly on the bed. "This where Richie slept?"

"Yeah."

She quit bouncing. "What grade was he in?"

"Third."

"What's in there?" She pointed at the box Mrs. Birk said so many other fosters had used. And she had accused *him* of asking too many questions. He was pleased, though, that now Ollie was taking her turn at being a pest.

"Stuff," he said.

"What kinda stuff?"

"Just stuff." David perched on the edge of his own bed. "Richie called 'em treasures. He liked to haul 'em to all the different places we lived." He was careful to make it sound as if he wasn't especially interested in any of them himself.

"Can I look at 'em?"

"No."

Ollie eyed the box as if she thought its lid would magically lift and the objects inside would levitate into the air before her eyes.

"I bet Richie wouldn't care if I did," she speculated.

"I would, though."

Ollie kept a lemon-lime stare fixed on the box.

"Okay! Okay!" David yelled. He folded his arms across his chest and studied the ceiling so that he wouldn't have to see any of the items Ollie was about to look at.

"Ummm, green glass," she murmured appreciatively. "I like the color green. Somebody—I can't remember who—gave me a green dress once. I was about seven, I think. It was practically new. I looked dumber'n a toad in it, but the color sure was pretty." She set the piece of glass on the windowsill in almost the exact spot Richie had put it.

She reached into the box again. "We could get eyes for this bear," she announced.

David allowed his gaze to drift slowly down from the ceiling.

"Toy stores sell eyes by the set or one at a time," Ollie said. "All sizes, all colors. Green eyes for cats, pink ones for rabbits, brown ones for dogs and bears. Probably aren't too expensive." She leaned the blind bear against the window frame.

"I don't aim to spend money I don't even have to buy eyes for a worthless old wore-out bear Richie got at the Goodwill for twenty-five cents," David heard himself declare.

"I got a dollar. I was saving up for cigarettes. I'll buy eyes," Ollie offered.

"What's this?" she wanted to know, holding up the

chrome hood ornament from the ancient, wrecked car in Uncle Paulie's weedy backyard.

He'd said he'd restore it someday and that it would be worth a small fortune when he sold it. "And when I get that money," Uncle Paulie said, "I'll buy you two guys your own bikes." He never got it fixed and there were never any bikes, but David had always liked that promise.

"It looks like something off a car," Ollie said.

"It is. A 1943 Pontiac Silver Streak."

"It makes a pretty statue." Ollie propped it next to the piece of green glass. She admired Prince Albert's faded portrait, and opened and shut the lid on the can until it quit squeaking. She held up Richie's yellow notebook. Richie had only used three pages in it; David had torn them out and thrown them away.

"Put that back," David ordered. She did.

"Richie had nice treasures," Ollie murmured, sighing. "I never bothered to collect anything. I mean, you can't be sure when the aid people are gonna come to get you again. Maybe I wouldn't have time to get my stuff all packed up. I'd feel worse'n ever if I had to leave any of my treasures behind."

"Tell me about it," David said. He thought he liked her a little better now. And he was glad she'd taken all the treasures out of the box and put them back on the windowsill. It was an investment in the future, but no way could he have made it himself.

"I got some fish and you still got Richie's treasures," Ollie said. "That's nice, David." He realized it was the second time she'd called him David.

Later, after she'd pulled the dresser in front of her door again, David wished he could tell Richie. It would

make him feel good if his brother knew that the treasures were back where they belonged. David crawled
into bed without getting undressed. The street lamp in
the alley glowed through the insulator cap and poured
a pool of pale green moonlight on the floor.

Richie, he began, Ollie's not too bad. You might even
like her. You know what she did today, Richie? She put
all your treasures back on the windowsill. She got in
trouble at school, though, and had to start going to
these classes with Evil Evan Ellis. . . .

What good were the words? No good at all. So why
bother with them? David turned his back to the window, and pulled the covers up around his ears.

Chapter Twelve

Two weeks later, Ollie wasn't quite as crabby when she got out of what she called CNC.

"CNC? What's that mean?" David wanted to know.

"Short for Conflict Negotiation Crap," she answered. "And you know how I feel about taking any of that stuff."

"You better not let Mr. Bateman hear you say what you just did," David warned.

Ollie gave him one of her Terrible Looks. He wondered sometimes if she practiced those looks in the mirror in the bathroom at the end of the hall at Mrs. Birk's. "So I should shake in my shoes?" She sniffed, then seemed to relent.

"Oh, I s'pose I can live with it," she admitted with a shrug when David asked her how the classes were going.

But he realized she seemed peculiar today; a soft dreaminess had replaced her Terrible Look and didn't fit her words.

And no matter what Ollie nicknamed the class, David was sure he'd noticed a change in Evil Evan Ellis, too. In

Mrs. Olson's room, Evan kept his stupid elephant feet under his own desk now. On the playground, he quit hanging out with his cronies, who draped themselves on the fence and regarded their former leader with anguished expressions of love gone sour. One day, when one of the first graders climbed up on the slide then got too scared to come down, Evil Evan actually lifted him to the ground, ruffling the kid's hair as if he were a puppy, a bemused smile on his own wide face.

David discovered on the way home, however, that it wasn't smooth progress in the CNC class that caused Ollie to stare into the distance and smile to herself.

"You hear about the school program?" she asked as they headed toward Mrs. Birk's. David hadn't.

"There's gonna be this talent assembly. In the gym. They're gonna fix up rows of chairs just like in a real theater. There's gonna be a stage and everything. Spotlights. Maybe even a curtain." Her words were as pensive and vague as Evan Ellis's smile.

"There's always something around Easter time," David observed. He'd seen lots of Easter programs in lots of different schools, and was sure Ollie must have, too. The fact that news of this one made her look dreamy and caused her sharp profile to soften as it cleaved into the spring air surprised him a little.

"A talent assembly," Ollie repeated, her voice airy with speculation. "Anybody can sign up. The sheet's pinned up on the bulletin board outside Mr. Bateman's office. I saw it."

Any school he'd ever gone to, there were always kids who knew how to play the piano, David reflected. Or the violin or the trumpet. Or could recite poems from memory. Such kids loved to show off in front of every-body else. As in other schools, some girls here at Franklin probably took dancing lessons. They would bring their ballet shoes to school and would have costumes made of netting and sequins in their hair.

Ollie was not that sort of a girl, of course.

"I signed up," Ollie murmured.

"You?"

She turned, the look on her face only mildly wrathful. "Yes, me," she said. "I'm going to sing."

David shuddered. He remembered the first day he'd ever seen her, when she'd straightened Mrs. Birk out about the name Olivia. "O-liv-ee-ya!" she'd screeched, and the room had filled to within an inch of the ceiling with boiling oil. Once, David was sure he'd heard her singing to Freddie, Frank, and Flo, and had sneaked across the hall to listen. The sound coming through the door had seemed scratchy and pained, though he wasn't able to make out the words.

"Sing?"

"Yeah. I like to sing."

Ollie obviously believed—mistakenly—that she sang well enough to be in a talent show, David realized.

"This one place I stayed, the fosters went to church. Every Sunday. The kind of church where people sing a lot. That's where I learned," she explained. "There was this one song I really loved. I especially liked the Sundays when it was one of the songs they picked."

"So sing it for me," David suggested. Maybe he was wrong; maybe she could sing after all.

"Hey, turkey. Didn't I have to practically beg you to see Richie's treasures? Sure I did. Well, now I'm not going to haul off and sing on command for *you*." Ollie stuck her chin out. "You can darn well wait till the assembly to hear me, just like everyone else."

While they ate apple slices with peanut butter in the kitchen, Ollie told Mrs. Birk about the talent show and that she planned to sing in it. Mrs. Birk had always seemed to be a calm person who took a reasonable, though not necessarily a deep, interest in school news, but this particular information enchanted her.

"A talent assembly! Oh, how lovely!" Her smile was wide and eager. Even more amazing, she became suddenly shy as soon as the words were out of her mouth.

"I don't know why, but most of the fosters Mr. Birk and I've had over the years were boys," she confessed. "There was only one girl—oh, she came a long time ago—and she was only able to stay for a few weeks."

Mrs. Birk continued to smile at Ollie as if seeing opportunities in her that had gone unnoticed till this moment. "Maybe I ought to sew you up something new," she said.

"Something new?" Ollie frowned. "Like what?"

"We could look through some magazines," Mrs. Birk suggested. "Or in that catalog that came in the mail the other day. The pictures are so nice, and I bet I could copy something for you if you picked out what you liked."

"No way could you make me look like most girls," Ollie pointed out. "Not that I want to," she added hastily. "People criticize my skinny legs all the time—call me Bones or Bird Legs—but my mama used to tell me I'm okay just the way I am."

Mrs. Birk was obviously a little disappointed, but she agreed. "Absolutely, dear. Your mama was right." David

realized that she'd really wanted to make Ollie something special for the talent assembly, though.

At bedtime, when Ollie was safely behind her barri-
caded door, David was sure he heard some sort of
singing going on across the hall. It sounded high and
thin and awful.

It would be better if Ollie didn't do this. People
would laugh at her, especially the girls. He wished he
could think of the right way to talk her out of it. Next
week, he decided, he'd try.

On the way to school on Monday, he did. "Maybe
you've got some other talent," he suggested. "Anyway,
you've got to have some accompaniment. You know,
someone to play the piano to get you started on your
song."

"No I don't. They didn't have a piano in that church
where those fosters took me. Those folks just hauled off
and sang. That's called a cappella, in case you don't
know. It means no piano, no nothing. Didn't *you* ever
go to church and sing a cappella?" Once again she was
her old, irritable self, and David felt reassured.

He realized he should have tried harder to dissuade
her, though, because the next afternoon after school
Ollie told Mrs. Birk that she was ready to look through
the Sears catalog.

"But I'm not the kind of person who's comfortable
getting all gussied up," she warned. "I don't want anything too nice. Or anything with lace."

"No lace," Mrs. Birk said eagerly, and scooted into
the living room to get the catalog from the shelf under
the TV.

"No ruffles either," Ollie called after her.

Mrs. Birk opened the catalog on the kitchen table and

Wendell sat underneath as they examined dresses in the junior girls' section. "No ruffles," Mrs. Birk agreed happily.

David pretended to read another chapter in *The World and Its People.* Long ago, in China, they bound up girls' feet to make it hard for them to walk. Such girls never ran away from home. It was a terribly painful practice, the book said, and David knew that Ollie would never have put up with that kind of treatment.

"Did I mention no bright colors either?" Ollie asked.

"What colors appeal to you, dear?" Mrs. Birk murmured as they leafed through page after page of dresses, skirts, and blouses. Ollie squinted with disapproval at most of the illustrations.

"Ummm, once I had this green dress. Like I told David, I looked dumber'n a toad in it, but the color sure was pretty."

"Yes, green would be good on you," Mrs. Birk murmured. "Redheads who have your eye color usually look splendid in green."

David had never thought of Ollie as a redhead— certainly not one who could look splendid. She had Gatorade eyes, and her hair was the color of those yarn wigs that clowns wear. How could such a girl look good in a dress? It worried him that Ollie, being so skinny, would look like a bundle of sticks wrapped in rags. Mrs. Birk plainly observed possibilities in her that he couldn't see himself.

At last the two of them seemed to agree on a style. David tried to see which dress it was, but there were several on the page and he couldn't decide which one they both liked. "Maybe I could get some material tomorrow," Mrs. Birk said.

"Nothing shiny. No fancy buttons. No bows," Ollie declared.

"Of course, dear." Mrs. Birk put a finger to her chin. "To make sure I don't make a mistake, perhaps we ought to pick the material out together. The mall is open until nine o'clock. Rather than wait, should we go tonight?"

David felt Mrs. Birk's glance rest on him. "We'll let David finish his lesson, and we'll be back before either he or Mr. Birk misses us."

David was disappointed to hear that he wasn't invited to the mall, too, and after watching a show on TV with Mr. Birk about how dolphins were accidentally getting caught in tuna nets and how nobody in the country should eat tuna anymore till the matter got straightened out, he went upstairs to his room, where he felt more excluded than ever.

He wished he could tell Richie about the whole crazy business. A girl who didn't even look much like a real girl and couldn't sing any better than Wendell was going to get dressed up and sing in front of the whole school. It would be a terrible disaster, and might end up making Ollie's life worse than ever. Her efforts in the negotiation classes would be wasted; the hoots and hollers that she'd get from the audience would make her so mean she'd be a menace to everyone on the school ground. Even teachers.

David hunched cross-legged on Richie's bed. Richie's smell was almost gone now, and he had to sniff deeply to retrieve the last remaining whiff.

He was about to call silently, Oh, Richie, come back, come back! when he heard the car pull into the driveway. Moments later, Ollie clumped up the stairs, her footfalls the two-hundred-pound variety again, and wandered into his room without being invited.

"We got you something," she announced.

"What?" David hoped Mrs. Birk didn't plan to sew him up something special too.

Ollie opened her fist. In her palm were two lovely, shiny eyes the color of honey. "Let's put 'em in, okay?"

She hadn't asked permission to come into his room and now she didn't ask permission to pick the bear up off the windowsill. She laid its shabby body across her knees and worked the new eyes—each had a sturdy, corkscrew-shaped pin attached to its back—into the bear's face in the two pale spots where the old eyes had been.

She examined her efforts. "Perfect. Someday maybe I'll be an eye surgeon," she declared with a smile.

David had preferred the bear when it couldn't see. Now, those honey-colored eyes surveyed the room, the hall, Richie's bed. Now, the bear knew Richie was gone. David tried not to think about that.

"What's the material for your dress like?" he asked to get his mind off the fact that now the bear would be a witness to everything.

"Not bad," Ollie said. "Sort of soft, like Bear-Bear's fur."

Were there no limits to the liberties she'd take? Without asking permission, she'd just given the bear a name! David was relieved when she jumped off the bed and headed toward her own room.

"Well, I gotta practice now," she announced. "See you in the morning."

Across the hall, it seemed to David that she didn't haul her dresser all the way across the door this time.

Soon he heard a muffled, vaguely musical sound. The words and tune were always too faint for him to understand anything clearly. He closed his own door, then could hear nothing at all.

Richie, David wished he could say, your bear knows now that you aren't here anymore. Should I take his eyes out so it won't bother him so much? Richie, what do *you* want me to do?

He waited a long time for a sign from Richie, but none ever came.

Chapter Thirteen

Every night as soon as the dishes were done, Mrs. Birk and Ollie retreated into Mrs. Birk's bedroom. Mrs. Birk kept her sewing machine there, and moved her ironing board from the kitchen so that she could press pieces of the new garment as it was assembled.

A lot of murmuring and trying on went on as they worked behind the almost-closed door. David knew about the trying on part because every so often he'd see Ollie's ragged Mickey Mouse sweatshirt get pitched aside, along with her holey jeans. Moments later, they would be retrieved by a skinny white arm whose elbow was sharper than a pirate's dagger.

They both seemed to enjoy what they were doing, but he didn't exactly enjoy watching TV alone with Mr. Birk, who had no more stories to tell about snakes at the UPS and often dozed off before most shows were over—even the exciting ones with three or four car chases and plenty of gunfire.

When Ollie and Mrs. Birk finally emerged, they usually looked pleased with each other, but kept details of the dress a secret between themselves.

On the morning of the assembly, David was disappointed that he wouldn't get to see their invention then either. Ollie was wearing an old coat when she came downstairs for breakfast, and ate her Choco Bits with it buttoned up around her neck as if the kitchen were freezing. It was April; he knew she couldn't be cold.

On the way to school, all he could spy was an edge of the dress peeking out below the frayed hem of her coat, which was ratty and in his opinion suited her better than anything new. What he could see didn't look green like grass or tree leaves, which was his idea of green, but seemed to be the funny gray-green color fruit gets when you leave it on top of the cupboard too long.

David remembered other assembly days in other schools. Such days, everyone got sort of goofy, as if a virus had been spread throughout the building via a faulty ventilating system. Even teachers were contaminated. From the way kids acted, you'd have thought everybody at Franklin had a special talent that he or she would display, that movie scouts from Hollywood were reported to be in the audience.

Evan Ellis—*Evan Ellis*, could you believe it?—was the master of ceremonies. He wore a pair of jeans so new you could hear the legs whisper every time he walked onto the stage. David could hear that sound from the back row, where he hunched on his folding chair in the twilit gloom of the half-darkened gym.

A few first graders were the first to perform. Next were the two kids who'd been on the playground the day Ollie smoked her final cigarette. One was dressed as a tomato and the other as a carrot. They recited a poem titled "Good Diet Means Don't Fry It."

A girl from third grade coaxed the cry of a grieving

cat out of her violin; someone from fourth was pretty good on an accordion that was bigger than he was.

It didn't surprise David a bit that Linda Lundy turned out to be one of those girls who'd taken dancing lessons. Margie Wade and Becky Love had, too, and the three of them got up on the stage in their costumes of what looked like butterfly netting, sequins sprinkled in their hair, to perform what was called a free dance. Being older than the first graders, though, it wasn't exactly as free as it was supposed to be because they were so self-conscious. At least Linda had been careful when she combed her hair, because it didn't stick out around her head like a giant yellow bush.

The reason he didn't truly enjoy any of the performances, David realized, was because Ollie obviously was scheduled to be last.

The ring of dampness around the back of his neck got wetter, and his stomach boiled. He sat on his hands, which made them stickier than ever. It was strange, he mused. He wasn't the one about to show off a talent, so why was *he* nervous?

The truth was, waiting in the audience for Ollie to appear in front of everyone was almost worse than knowing he had to get onstage himself. Alone in the half-darkness (he felt alone even though most of his class sat in the same row he did, and Mrs. Olson was right across the aisle), he had too much time to worry about a person who—even though she was still more or less a stranger to him—was going to make a total ass out of herself before the morning was over.

The gym was oddly silent when Ollie finally stepped from behind a curtain someone's mother had made out of an old chenille bedspread that was dyed dark blue for the occasion.

David suspected the quietness of the audience was due partly to the fact that everyone knew the assembly was just about over but mostly because (he knew this in his gut) they all looked forward to how outrageous Ollie would be.

He was only slightly relieved to discover her dress was exactly what Ollie had specified. It had no ruffles, no lace. No buttons, no bows; it wasn't shiny either. It wasn't a dress as much as it was a tunic such as a page in King Arthur's court might have worn. It hung straight to her knees, and in the light shining down on her it was the same silver-green color as the underside of an oak leaf.

Her rusty knees weren't visible at all because Mrs. Birk had gotten a pair of tights almost the same shade as the dress. The bill on Ollie's baseball cap was gone (how come he hadn't noticed this earlier, when they'd left the house?). Her hair, tamed with some sort of lotion Mrs. Birk must have put on it, hugged her head like a burnished medieval helmet.

Ollie opened her mouth.

David closed his ears.

He squinched his eyes shut tight.

He knew what was coming next would be horrible. So embarrassing that he'd want to die in her place. He gritted his teeth, hardening himself against the hisses and jeers that in moments would wash across the gym like a tidal wave.

He tried to think of what he'd say to her when they walked home this afternoon after school. Her stony heart, impervious to grief, would be broken. She'd be so humiliated that she might even cry. On second thought, he wasn't sure if anything could make her do that.

The first sounds he heard were round and smooth, like marshmallows that have been blackened over a campfire, then had their outer layers peeled away. Round and smooth. Plain and perfect.

David opened his eyes.

"Amazing grace how sweet the sound,
    That saved a wretch like me. . . ."

The words were sort of familiar. Somewhere, maybe he'd heard them before. But when Ollie sang the word *wretch* it didn't sound wretched at all. The sound was . . . Oh, it was like a blessing, an acceptance of pain and grief that unclamped his bowels and massaged his chest with strong, warm fingers.

"I once was lost but now am found,
    Was blind, but now I see. . . ."

Lost . . . but found. Blind . . . but see. Round, plain, perfect words.

The words and sounds floated, singly and in pairs, over the heads of everyone in the half-darkened gym, messengers on little wings. Moths, velvet-bodied, soft-eyed, that rose into the rafters of the gym and circled, circled. Below, no feet shuffled. No one sneezed. Nobody coughed. No one hissed.

"Through many dangers, toils, and snares,
    I have already come. . . ."

David wiped his hands on his jeans. Richie, can you hear?

> "'Tis grace that brought me safe thus far,
>   And grace will lead me home. . . ."

Ollie kept her eyes fastened on some point above the heads turned up to her in the mellow gloom, on something that perhaps only she knew was there.

Was she remembering those happy Sundays in church with those other fosters? David wondered. Was she thinking about all the funerals she'd gone to, even the one where no sandwiches were served? Did she reflect on catsup and Evan Ellis, about calling Mr. Hutton and telling him she was going to hit the road, on her famous motto and everything she'd learned in that CNC class?

David couldn't attach himself to all the words, but certain ones seemed meant only for him. "Bright shining as the sun . . ." Richie's yellow notebook, the color of the sun—at this moment was it glowing in the darkness of the treasure box under the windowsill upstairs at Mrs. Birk's? Did its unblemished pages hold some sort of secret message for him?

The last words and notes of Ollie's song were more perfect and plain than the first ones.

> "We've no less days to sing God's praise,
>   Than when we'd first begun."

When she was finished, she didn't leave the stage right away. She smiled. David knew she was smiling to herself, not to anyone in the audience.

When she turned to leave, her profile was as keen as the prow of a ship against the dark curtain behind her. Her legs were bent slightly at the knees. She leaned forward into a wind that blew lightly along a beach near some invisible ocean.

Oh, Richie! David cried. I wish you could've been here this morning because that girl I told you about remember her name's Ollie well she sang this song she told me it was a cappella that means no piano no nothing about being a wretch and having something amazing happen and how you could get lost then found again and somewhere there's grace and the sun's still shining Richie oh Richie . . . !

Chapter Fourteen

After Saturday chores were finished a week later, on an afternoon when the few new leaves on the tree in front of the Birks' porch were almost the same color as the dress David never saw Ollie wear again, she settled herself at the kitchen table.

David watched as she piled some materials beside her. A stack of paper Mrs. Birk had given her, pencils, an eraser, a box of crayons. He knew she had only one session left in her conflict negotiation class; she must have an important final report to hand in next Friday. He was eager to hear what she'd been assigned to write about.

Ollie smoothed a sheet in front of her, and drew her brows together. Her hair had returned to its former untamed condition. She put a pencil in her mouth and nibbled on it.

"I've got this idea," she announced.

David sat across the table from her. Her voice didn't sound much like broken glass anymore. "For your CNC class next week?" he asked.

He'd noticed other, more subtle differences about her now that she was sort of famous. Among other things, since the talent assembly everyone at school regarded her with curious respect, and she'd taken to talking to Evan Ellis in the hallway. They gave each other shy, astonished looks, but never talked too long nor stood too close.

"Let's write to Richie."

David stared at her. Fame had affected her mind.

"Don't be an idiot," he said.

Ollie paid no attention to him and began to write.

"Listen. Richie never was much of a reader," David warned. "The alphabet was all mixed up for him. He couldn't always tell certain letters apart. Like for Richie, m's looked the same as w's, b's looked like d's or h's, and g's were the same as p's and q's."

David waited for her to put her pencil down.

Instead, she printed the date at the top of her paper.

"Richie . . . he's . . . *gone!*" David yelled. He realized he was fiercely warm all over.

"Doesn't matter," Ollie said in the same airy tone she'd used when she informed him she'd signed up for the talent assembly. "Main thing is, Richie will know we're writing to him."

"He can't know!" David hollered louder. "Didn't you hear what I just told you? Richie . . . I mean, he's *my* brother, after all. I ought to know more about him than you do. You didn't even live here when he . . . and what I'm telling you is . . . he's gone." He enunciated each word slowly and carefully, as if she were an old person who was hard of hearing. "Gone to a place where you can't send people letters." Most certainly that fact would get her attention.

It was as if Ollie were truly deaf and hadn't heard a thing he'd said.

"Dear Richie," she murmured, printing carefully as she spoke. "Today David and I are going to write letters to you."

"I am not!" David yelped. He felt warmer than ever. The cool column in his middle (it had never completely disappeared) suddenly began to melt, just like whenever people were too nice or called him "dear."

"Of course, you don't know me," Ollie continued. "My name's Olivia Rose Nickleby. Everybody calls me Ollie. It's a name that always seemed to suit me better than Olivia. Someday I might change my mind about that, though."

"Stop!" David screeched.

"I'm staying for a while at the same house where your brother, David, still lives. You know, with the Birks. I'm in the room across the hall from where you used to be."

"Quit that!" David warned. His face and ears were scorched. He felt like one of those people he'd seen pictures of who pour molten steel out of huge dippers then flatten it into sheets in mills in Pittsburgh.

He glared at her. In addition to being demented, she was a cruel, hateful person. Talking to Richie as if she had a right to. She didn't. No way. Now, he wondered how she could have made those notes come out so round and perfect at the talent thingamajig.

He'd get even with her. He'd stick something slimy in her bed. Yeah. A fresh batch of Wendell's doo-doo from the backyard.

Now that she wasn't pulling the dresser in front of her door anymore he'd sneak in there—soon, maybe tonight—and cut off all her ugly frizzy orange clown hair. She'd have to go to school looking like a convict.

He'd peek at her through the keyhole when she took her bath, and tomorrow he'd tell Evan Ellis he'd seen her naked.

"David said you liked Wendell a lot," Ollie wrote on. "I do too. He's smart, for a dog. Why, do you know what Wendell told me yesterday, Richie? That he misses you, that's what, and he hopes you're doing okay in that place you're at now."

She claimed Wendell had talked to her yesterday?

It was too much.

David scooped up her papers, pencils, the eraser, the box of crayons, and swept everything into the air in a delirious flurry.

For an instant, the kitchen was filled with flying debris. It all fell, not very noisily, onto the floor. Ollie studied the mess, gathered it up without a word, sorted and stacked it all neatly, put the crayons back in their box, set everything on the table again. She leaned across it and looked him in the eye.

"This happens to be my foster home too," she advised him in steely tones. "I'll sit here and write to Richie if I darn well feel like it. You got that, turkey?" Now she was the old Ollie, the one with a peel-the-paint-off-the-wall voice and eyes like battery acid.

David sat down, faintly reassured.

Ollie wrote steadily, mouthing her text so softly to herself that David could only make out a phrase now and then.

". . . last week I sang in school. . . . Wendell got his distemper shot. . . . Isn't life a surprise? . . . You are there. . . . I am here. . . ."

David reached for a piece of paper.

It was clean and white on one side but had writing

on the other side. Mrs. Birk said it was a sin to throw paper away that still had one good side left. If a person used it, she said, it meant another tree wouldn't have to be cut down in a forest somewhere in South America.

He picked up a pencil.

He looked at the paper for a long time. Across the table, Ollie's pencil squeaked steadily across her page.

"Dear Richie," David began. The minute he started, the words tumbled onto the page so fast that he couldn't get them arranged properly or be bothered by periods and commas.

"Oh Richie oh I miss you Richie and I wish you'd never eaten that stupid pizza but I want to explain the reason why I never went to your funeral see it was because I just couldn't even though I knew I'd feel awful afterward so I just stayed upstairs and sniffed your bedspread Richie because everything seemed kind of hopeless on account of Mrs. Birk's purse looked so black and ugly squatting there on her knees see it made me think about what it would be like to be in a coffin no no Richie I just couldn't. . . ."

He crumpled up the paper and started again.

"Dear Richie. Listen. It's me. Your brother, David. Well, I shouldn't have told you we'd never get split up. It turned out to be a lie. Only I didn't know it at the time, Richie. I figured I was telling you the truth. I believed it as much as you."

"I think we should go see your brother next week," Ollie said, interrupting his train of thought.

"See him? We can't see Richie," David said.

There was no doubt about it now. She *was* crazy. "That's the dumbest of all your dumb, stupid, ignorant ideas," David heard himself whisper. He couldn't seem to dial up much volume in his voice. He had been almost ready to forgive her, was writing letters like she wanted, now here she was ruining things again.

"Of course we can see him. I mean, we can see where Richie's at now."

"I'm not going to any cemetery."

"But I want you to," Ollie said matter-of-factly, folding her letter in half, then in half again.

"Your idea about these letters was crazy enough!" David yelled. He was glad that, even though it was misting lightly outdoors, Mrs. Birk had put on her rain hat and had gone out to putter with her irises next to the driveway.

"You wanted me to write a letter so I did! But we can't send them to Richie, you boneheaded brainless booger! We can't because . . . because . . . Richie's dead."

Richie's dead. There. He'd said it. Had finally hooked that name and that word together. They would never come apart again. They were cemented to each other for all time. *Richie's dead.*

"Right. So that's why we have to go to the cemetery," Ollie murmured. "Because that's where Richie's at, and because it's the only place we can take his letters." She decorated the remaining white space on the outside of hers with red, yellow, and blue flowers that she drew with crayon. She entwined them with bunches of green leaves.

"I know where it's at too, because when me and Mrs. Birk went to the mall to get the material for that dress, she showed me. If you'd gone to your brother's funeral, you'd know too."

Oh, Richie! David apologized silently, I wanted to go

but I just couldn't because I didn't want to think of you that way and I figured if I didn't see where they put you it was like you weren't really gone then I'd wake up some morning and you'd be in the bed across from me and all the treasures would be on the windowsill and the bridges and roads and mountains would still be in the corner of the backyard and I wouldn't know anything about this crazy person named Ollie and you and me would be together like always oh Richie!

"We can take Wendell with us," Ollie said. "Of course, we'll have to put him on a leash. Dogs aren't allowed in cemeteries"—she raised her eyebrows—"for obvious hygienic reasons. We'll wait until we get an almost-perfect day, though. Sometimes a cemetery can be a sad place, so it's a good idea to visit when it's nice. Until a person gets used to it."

David felt weak. He let his chin drop almost level with the tabletop. "You mean we have to go more than once?"

Ollie looked up, surprised. "Well, sure. I mean, that's where Richie's at now, right?"

David felt the remainder of the cool column in his middle melt away completely. It drained out through a hole in the big toe of his left foot.

Wendell walked along respectfully, not leaning forward on his leash, eager to tear off among the headstones, or straining to lift his leg wherever he felt inspired to. The air was peculiarly warm, and David's insides felt clean and uncluttered now that the ice in his center was gone.

Ollie carried the letters. David regretted that his flowers weren't as pretty as hers, that his leaves were blobs.

"How will we know where he's at?" he asked. Unfortunately, his voice had that familiar thin-as-a-shoelace sound in it again.

"I asked Mrs. Birk for directions. She drew me sort of a little map. I don't think we'll have any trouble." Ollie consulted a piece of paper she took out of her hip pocket.

"The places are probably alphabetized," David speculated. "All we need to do is find where they put the *H*'s."

Ollie gave him a disgusted look. "People don't die in alphabetical order, David."

Richie's place was small, and seemed to fit him.

The headstone that was laid flat in the grass had a small rose etched on it. Richie's name was carved beside it. There was something so different about the way it looked all spelled out that way: *Richard Avery Haywood.*

It was as if Richie had had a history as long as anyone else's; had died, without regret, of something ordinary. David imagined Richie old: His hair would be pale, gone-to-seed dandelion tufts like Gramma's. His glasses would be smudged. He would smell partly sweet and partly sour.

Ollie sat cross-legged on the grass, and Wendell lay beside her. She placed the letters in a metal frame above the headstone that David figured was intended to hold flowers.

"Well, Richie, we're here," she said. "I want to say I wish I'd known you before, well, you know, before that business with the pizza."

The sunlight slanting through the thin-leafed tree branches was lemon-colored. David turned his gaze away from the stone. "Are you sure Richie can hear us?" he whispered.

"Ummm. I think so," Ollie told him.

Now that he was finally here, a fresh and terrifying thought occurred to David.

"What if Mr. Hutton comes to get me tomorrow?" he agonized aloud. "What if I get moved again, a long way from here? What if I have a hard time getting back to visit Richie?"

Ollie squinted, and brushed her hair from her brow. "I got this theory," she said.

David wasn't surprised. After all, she'd had mottoes and ideas; that she also had a theory seemed fitting.

"Like, there's some things you and me can't change. Getting stuck in foster care. What happened to Richie. The way I look. Stuff like that." When she turned to him, David saw that the pale sun through her lashes cast frail, spiky shadows across her cheeks. He realized he liked the way she looked.

"But wherever you are, that's where you've got to be. I mean really *be*." Those were a lot like the words he'd used himself when he and Richie looked down on the Birks' backyard from the upstairs window for the first time. David wasn't surprised to learn that Ollie had carried the idea further than he had.

"I don't mean that where you are is just a place you're at. See, it's more than just a location. Wherever you are, that's where you got to do your living. Dream your dreams. Find your"—she hesitated—"your grace. You have to make stuff work for you *where you're at*, not where you wish you were."

David wondered if this was something she'd learned in the class with Evan Ellis. Maybe it was the same theory that made Evan lift that first grader off the slide and ruffle the little guy's hair.

"Richie's wherever he is, and today we're right here with him. Not anyplace else. Maybe we should be glad about that. Instead of worrying about Mr. Hutton or what might happen tomorrow."

David remembered what hard work it had always been to be. Maybe now it would get easier, even though Richie was gone. The thought soothed him.

"You and me both know everything will change, right?"

Right, David agreed silently.

"Today, though, here we are. You and me. Wendell also. We wrote letters to Richie. Later, when we get moved again, we can always remember what we did today." Ollie sighed. "Well, that's my theory."

David wondered if he should ask her to sing that song again, the one about amazement and being lost then found again. He could still clearly hear those round, smooth, perfect marshmallow sounds in his head.

To be silent was almost as good, though, so he allowed himself to drift, as beguiled by the moment as Ollie seemed to be. He thought of Richie's notebook, the color of the sun, glowing in the dark at the bottom of Mrs. Birk's treasure box. He would take it out. He might begin to write in it. Tonight, maybe, before he went to sleep. Words for Richie. Discoveries for himself.

"It's Saturday," Ollie announced after a while. David blinked. He'd known that all day, hadn't he? "And you know what happens on Saturday."

David tried to remember. "Mrs. Birk makes cookies," he said. She did most of her baking for the whole week on Saturday afternoon, and it seemed to him that Wendell smiled when he heard the word *cookies*.

"We can come here again next week if we decide to," Ollie said.

"Give me the map just in case sometime I want to come by myself," David suggested. Now, such a thing was possible. Yes; soon he'd want to come here alone so that it could be just him and Richie for a little while. Like always. Ollie plucked the map from her pocket. David put it into his own.

When they passed through the cemetery gate, they let Wendell off his leash. Even now, he didn't plunge recklessly ahead, but seemed content to walk sedately at Ollie's heel, as if himself reflecting on the importance of the visit they'd just made. Shadows from the partly leafed, partly bare branches overhead patterned the sidewalk with lace, and David realized that the awful space between his collarbone and belly button felt nearly normal.

"When we get home I'll have to clean out the bowl for Freddie, Frank, and Flo," Ollie said, and scuffed her feet lightly on the sidewalk. Most of the time lately she seemed to weigh only about seventy-five pounds.

"After that, you want to build some bridges and roads and rivers in the backyard?" David asked.

In the afternoon light, Ollie's green glance was mild. David couldn't imagine why it had once reminded him of battery acid.

"Why not?" she asked. Her smile was easy and agreeable. For the first time in longer than he could remember, David felt the corners of his own mouth turn up too.